James King's

JUNGLE JIM

Shadows and the of Kinabalu

Matador
9 Priory Business Park,
Wistow Road, Kibworth Beauchamp,
Leicestershire. LE8 0RX
Tel: 0116 279 2299
Email: books@troubador.co.uk
Web: www.troubador.co.uk/matador
Twitter: @matadorbooks

ISBN 978 1784624 972

British Library Cataloguing in Publication Data.
A catalogue record for this book is available from the British Library.

Matador is an imprint of Troubador Publishing Ltd

Contents

01. The
FLYING COFFIN

Somewhere over the South China Sea...

Fierce winds buffeted the small plane as it flew through inky black storm clouds. The plane was called *The Flying Coffin*, and right now its passengers took no comfort in the aircraft's unfortunate name. Forks of purple lightning flashed all around them as the 14-seater Douglas DC-2 propeller plane valiantly tried to stay on its course towards the jungle-clad island of Borneo. Continual bouts of turbulence made this virtually impossible and the ride was fast becoming an aerial roller coaster. The pilot tried to clear the condensation from the windshield with an already damp rag as he searched for landmarks through the rain-soaked glass. His face was ashen as he tried to suppress the fear that was rising from the pit of his stomach. The storm intensified as grey sheets of rain lashed the fuselage and pummelled the windows, obscuring the plane's forward propeller from view.

As another bolt of lightning struck the plane, Jim peered

through the rivulets running horizontally across the window closest to him and tried to keep his cool. He focused instead on the tattered remains of an old map that he clutched in his left hand. Written on it was the single word *Help!* in a familiar feminine scrawl, and an X placed over an unknown location.

Hang on, Ruthie, thought Jim. *I'm coming!*

As he tucked the map fragment safely back into his pocket, Jim instinctively glanced at the eerie spider tattoo inscribed on the palm of his hand. He had acquired it a few years back, while on holiday in Thailand. Curiously, he had no conscious recollection of having had the ink tattooed into his skin, or of ever particularly wanting a tattoo.

To his utter astonishment, Jim had quickly discovered that whatever he touched or held in his right hand thereafter didn't move, almost as though he had some sort of super-glue grip! The strength in his grip became useful as he never dropped or accidentally let go of anything he didn't mean to. It shocked him at first, but as time passed and he grew used to it, Jim decided that he liked this inexplicable new power and used it to his advantage as he wielded his hockey stick on the ice with strength and determination. Besides, it made him unique – and that was a trait Jim had always desired… to be ultimately famous one day, to be loved for what he was good at. He had shown his best friend Rufus McFly the tattoo when he'd returned to England and set him the task of researching the unusual arachnid design. When Rufus failed to unearth anything conclusive, Jim put it out of his mind and tried to focus on his game as a star ice-hockey player. But he was determined that one day he would uncover the mystery of the strange tattoo and its astonishing powers.

Rufus was sitting next to him now, staring out of his own window while trying not to panic. *And making a very bad job of it*, thought Jim. Safely stowed behind them were their bags; Rufus' containing his equipment, camera, torch, pens and paper, while Jim's was jam-packed with jungle survival gear as well as two very important items. Jim never travelled anywhere without his special hockey stick and his favourite hockey puck, which was labelled 'The Stroke of Luck'. His friend Ruthie had accidentally hit him in the face with it, giving him a long scar over his left eye. He was angry with her at the time, but as it healed he grew to like the scar as it made him look different. *I'm coming, Ruthie*, he thought, staring again at the cry for help scrawled on the map. *I'm on my way.*

Jim had been a star player for the Soho Wasps, England's best junior ice-hockey team, for several years alongside school, until an ankle injury had cut short his career. Since then Jim had been recovering and searching for something else to do, something to make him feel as important and valued as he once did. For some time, especially recently, he had felt like he lacked purpose. He wanted desperately to feel special again – at the very least to himself.

Jim glanced out of the window and came crashing back into reality. He saw what he could only describe as a funnel of black water towering over the small plane, ready to engulf it any second. The weather-beaten DC-2 tried to swerve, but the pilot struggled with the controls trying to evade this mysterious and malevolent force of nature, which, impossibly, seemed to be following them.

Jim heard the pilot curse as there was a sudden upward lurch. The plane barely missed the jagged, jungle-lined cliff that seemed to loom from nowhere. Jim felt his stomach roll, the plane seemed to move in slow motion as the water in his drinking cup floated in midair like a jellyfish for a few long seconds. *Urg–?* Then the water splashed against the back of the chair in front of him.

Next to Jim, Rufus was holding onto his seat for dear life. A super intelligent academic bookworm more at home in libraries and the streets of urban London, Rufus was on this mission because he possessed an encyclopedic knowledge of places and cultures that Jim knew he would need as he journeyed through Borneo. Dressed in casual clothes, with trendy round glasses and a mop of wavy black hair, Rufus was the opposite of Jim in almost every respect. While Jim was tall and sporty, every inch the ice hockey pro, Rufus was smaller and slight – the most exercise he got was opening and closing dusty old books and climbing ladders in libraries. Right now Rufus had turned pale and was digging his fingers into the worn blue leather padding of his seat.

"You okay, Rufus?" said Jim, trying to keep it together himself.

"Oh-oh-ok as I will ever be when faced with i-i-imminent death!" squeaked Rufus, the terror raising his voice a few notches.

"It can't be far now," replied Jim

"I-I hope we land soon," said Rufus, "or I might throw up! Do we even know where we are?"

As the plane banked to the right Jim could make out the silhouette of a densely packed jungle and giant trees in the eerie darkness below. Flashes of lightning gave him glimpses of what lay ahead. "There's a jungle below us, but I don't see anywhere we can land."

The cabin lights flickered as Jim looked around. He swallowed nervously.

"I think we might be in trouble..." muttered Jim as he stared desperately out into the darkness.

Rain and clouds swirled around as the propellers left tornado-like eddies in their path. An evil laugh, almost hidden in the thunder, rumbled on the wind. Storm clouds churned and lightening forked pink across the boiling sky, and for a fleeting second the elements resolved themselves into a gigantic pair of serpent eyes that seemed to be looking directly at Jim, and then they were gone. Rubbing his eyes, Jim looked out the window again and shook his head. "Great, now I'm seeing things," he said to himself. "Keep it together, Jim Regent! This is reality, not a movie!"

Just then, several red lights started flashing erratically on the ceiling of the plane while a deafening alarm echoed through the tiny cabin. He could hear the pilot saying something in the cockpit, but all the noise prevented him from hearing what it was. The engine bolted to the left wing was struck by a fork of lightning and was glowing with static as electricity surged through the plane. The driveshaft snapped in an explosion of sparks and squealing metal, sheering the propeller like an out of control band saw. It spun wildly, slicing through the main fuselage and separating Jim and Rufus from the cockpit. As the pilot screamed, the friends looked at each other in horror as they saw the front of the plane slowly disappear.

A second later, they passed out.

✪

Blinking and holding his head in pain, as if he'd been struck from behind, Jim reached up and felt the wind and rain scouring his face.

"Urg!" Jim's stomach dropped as he realised they had started falling toward the dark storm-ridden jungle below. He turned to Rufus, who was unconscious in his seat. As packing boxes and loose luggage fell from what was left of the ceiling, Jim began to look around for a way out. He reached under his seat and his hand clasped around what felt like a parachute. He tugged on it and it came free; stained and dirty, it had clearly seen better days. *I hope this thing still works*, thought Jim as he began to open all the straps.

Before Jim could worry further, the plane was hit by another bolt of lightning, causing it to spin out of control. Jim was thrown back into his seat, and the parachute slipped from his hand, whirling into the dark sky beyond his reach, the straps waving goodbye as they flapped and shrank into the distance.

"Oh, no!" Now truly panicked, Jim unbuckled himself from his seat, and then did the same for Rufus, who slumped forward. Jim held on tight. "Hold on, pal! We have to get out of this plane alive. We can't give up now!"

Reaching under Rufus' seat, Jim pulled the last parachute loose and began to strap it around his chest and shoulders. He felt the straps snap closed, then wrestled Rufus' body into a bear hug, clasping his strong, muscled arms around his friend's limp body. He grabbed their bags, his hockey stick protruding from one end, and placed them around his neck.

"Here goes!" Jim and the unconscious Rufus piled forwards, bashing and crashing past the remaining seats to suddenly find themselves tumbling as one, like a stone, and finally being sucked out of the front of the disintegrating plane, which was plummeting toward the rapidly rising jungle floor. Jim stole a glance behind him and watched in awe as the damaged plane crashed through the tall treetops and exploded in a fireball.

Hahahahahahahahahahaha!

As they fell Jim heard a sinister cackle echo through his mind, making his vision go dark just for a second. But he didn't have time to dwell on strange voices as he reached with his free hand and pulled on the parachute's toggle. It opened with a loud *Fwoomp!* – and there was a jolt as Jim was yanked upward. He suddenly lost his grip on Rufus, and watched in horror as his best friend began to slip through his rain soaked arms and fall like a rag doll toward the dark jungle canopy below.

"Rufus! *Noooooooooo!*"

Jim could only watch in despair as his best friend disappeared from sight. Tears welled in his eyes and a heavy lump in his chest made it hard to breathe.

✪

As Jim drifted toward the jungle, all he could hear was the wind rushing past and the endless rain pelting the trees below. Still recovering from a multitude of shocks, he could not help but ask himself: *what just happened?* He had never lost his grip like that before, especially when he used his right hand – the one with the spider tattoo. If he used that hand he had an unshakeable grip on anything he touched or held. But how had he lost his grip on Rufus?

Rufus! A surge of sadness filled his eyes with tears, which streamed down his face with the rain.

Surely he could not have survived the fall? He must have plunged hundreds of metres to the jungle floor.

"RUFUS!" he roared, but it didn't matter how loud he shouted the name, Jim knew no one could survive that fall. Despair was setting in and all he could do was float down, down, down into the darkness, the last parachute billowing above his head. But a tiny glimmer of hope flickered in the depths of his heart. His best friend had survived and was all right. *Rufus had to be alive? Didn't he?*

His thoughts were interrupted by the sound of breaking foliage as he finally came into contact with the jungle canopy. The trees cut and scratched him as he fought his way through their huddled mass. His parachute caught on a large branch as he jolted to a sudden stop. Jim barely had a second to look up in confusion before the canvas finally gave way and he plummeted towards the ground in a tangle of duffle bags and cords.

"Aargh!" Suddenly Jim stopped falling. An immense pain stabbed through his side as he landed on a giant twisted branch. Jim tried to focus. Where was he? The sound of insects was like an intense electrical discharge piercing his mind. The rain-soaked darkness seemed to swallow him, smother him with black shadows flitting in and out of the surrounding jungle. Gingerly, he touched his side. Pain shot through him like a bullet. He drew his hand away and squinted. His palm was red with his blood.

Things were getting desperate.

02. Prey of the
MANTIS

"Rufus!" cried Jim. "Rufus!" It was pointless. The mind numbing, ear-piercing din of the insects was deafening.

After catching his breath for a few minutes and wrapping a makeshift bandage around the wound on his side, Jim decided it was too dangerous to stay put. Looking down from his perch, he guessed he was only about ten metres above the jungle floor. The rain and thunder had not abated, and as he started to climb down to the ground, Jim winced in pain. The fall had battered him and possibly even broken a few of his ribs. His head blazed with searing pain and a flash vision of those sinister snake eyes appeared before him and then dissolved into the darkness once again.

What on earth is going on? Jim's mind raced as he painfully made his way down to the muddy jungle floor. *What IS this place?* When he reached the ground he began to scan the area, trying to make sense of the rain-obscured dark. He could smell burning fuel mixed with the dankness of rotting vegetation. In the distant sky he saw flames and billowing smoke, and he knew that was all that was left of the plane. He reached down and patted the duffle bag that contained his lucky puck and hockey stick, glad he had pulled it with him from the plane.

Again, he began to shout Rufus' name – but there was too much noise and chaos for him to be heard. He turned around in a circle, trying to think what Rufus would do were he in this situation.

"Think, Regent!" said Jim aloud, slapping his forehead. "Rufus is a clever guy. What would he do?" He laughed sadly and added, "Rufus would never have put himself in this situation to begin with." Jim sighed and steeled himself, trying to muster his confidence and hold onto that glimmering hope: Rufus was alive and well. He just *had* to be.

Jim's usually immaculately styled reddish brown hair was by now so drenched it was plastered to his face and getting in his eyes, and as he pushed it away he felt the scar over his left eye, which filled him with courage. His combat trousers were torn and his army boots coated in thick heavy mud, but Jim just shouldered the two bags and started off in the direction of the burning plane.

The more he walked, the harder it became for him to see in the wet blackness of the jungle. He called out Rufus' name from time to time, but there was no response. After battling through whipping leaves and spiky fern-like plants with barbed tentacles, Jim needed to stop and catch his breath. He reached out and rested his arm on what he thought was a tree branch – but it was covered in fine, prickly hairs.

"What the–?" said Jim, but he was interrupted by a loud screech.

"*KREEEEEEEEEEEEEE!*"

As lightning flashed he saw that what he tried to lean on was no tree branch. He was face to face with the drooling mandibles of a house-sized praying mantis! The monster bug opened its huge jaws, and, clicking and screeching, lunged at Jim. Astonished, Jim quickly ducked to the side – and only narrowly missed being devoured.

"Whoa! What is this, *Jurassic Park*?" exclaimed Jim, as he scrambled to pull his hockey stick from his duffle bag. He brandished the stick in front of him and yelled at the giant creature. "You want to fight? *Let's fight!*"

✪

Rufus lay on what felt to him like a soft, warm bed. It was very comfortable, aside from the growing pain in his legs. All he remembered was passing out on the plane, and then he woke up here, wherever here was.

What a horrible nightmare, he thought, his memories swimming into focus. *Where am I?* A strange red light glowed all around him, and an intense smell of rotting meat filled his nostrils. What felt like tentacles were slowly moving up his legs, causing them to burn.

"Ouch!" cried Rufus, his eyes opened wide then instinctively shut. They hurt!

The air was humid, heavy and acrid, and as he struggled to move, he could see that he wasn't in bed at all, but encased in what looked like red and white wrinkled flesh. There were long yellow tentacles curling around his arms and legs. Rufus suddenly felt a burning fear trace up his spine as something coiled around his head. A yellow, sinuous tentacle wrapped itself around his mouth as Rufus attempted to let out a scream.

Trying to fight against the quickly constricting prison, he flailed as much as he could, punching and grabbing with his free hands. He heard a pop and then a fiery liquid began to engulf him. The last thing he saw was a shadow against the glowing red and white walls – and then he heard a sharp noise…

But within seconds he could breathe again, and he felt long spindly hands reach for him and pull him from his fleshy tomb. He still could not see much as he was coated with the yellow, sticky goo – but he could make out what looked like the body of a skinny tribesman and the flash of eyes in the darkness now that the red light had faded. He took a welcome breath of air and passed out, caught by a pair of slender but immensely strong arms.

14

✪

Jim stood before the massive praying mantis in a fighting stance, his hockey stick held before him. The mantis reared up and took a swipe at him with one of its long bladed forearms. The mutant insect was fast! Jim was scared but saw his moment to run just after dodging another large, razor-sharp pincer.

He bolted from the creature but as soon as he ran a few steps he knew he would not get far, as the ground was sodden and covered by a thick layer of wet leaves and mulch. He skidded across the leaves for several seconds as if he was on ice, and then crashed into a jumble of tree roots, which spread across the ground like veins from the towering rocket-finned trees. Jim fell and went tumbling down a steep slope.

The mantis was right behind him, its massive strides outweighing his small ones ten to two. It towered above the slope as Jim edged backward against a giant slippery tree root and tried to find cover behind it. Above him, the mantis rose up and screeched.

"*KREEEEEEEEEE!*"

Jim laughed at the creature. "That got you, you giant... *bug!*" But as soon as Jim had spoken those words the mantis flew into the air on vast, whirring wings and swooped down the slope. "Man, do you ever give up?" he shouted in exasperation. Jim knew he was in trouble and started running once more.

15

Stealing a quick look behind him, Jim saw the mantis move nimbly across the wet ground towards him as if the dense jungle and twisted plant life were not even there. Jim's path was treacherous underfoot, and an army of plants and branches tried to claw at his body with barbs and needles. Dodging the swipes of the mantis' pincers from behind, Jim ignored the pain and pushed himself to keep going. *I can't die like this,* he thought. *Not alone and wounded in this hellish place!*

After what seemed like an eternity sliding and running amongst twisted vines and tree roots, Jim dived headlong into a dense patch of undergrowth and used his hockey stick to slash at the giant leaves and plants, slicing a path ahead for himself. He hit something solid and the hockey stick flew out of his hands as a shockwave of pain surged through his arms. Shaking out the pain, he picked up his hockey stick and glanced back to make sure the praying mantis was no longer on his tail. Brushing aside the giant sodden leaves, he jumped back in shock when he saw a terrifying face carved into a large tree trunk. A bat flew out of the face's mouth, startling him once again.

Clearing the rest of the leaves away, Jim could see that the tree was massive, reaching high up into the sky, and covered with intricate tribal carvings. A warm glow seemed to emanate from behind the tree, as Jim clambered around its base he came upon a large open area bathed in flickering firelight and surrounded by dozens of similarly carved trees. In the centre of the circle towered a huge statue carved from wood. It was an orangutan. The figure was ornate and weird, but Jim felt himself strongly drawn to it. As he wondered who carved it and why it was here, he did not hear the rustle of leaves and undergrowth behind him – until it was too late.

"OOF!" Jim was hit from behind and knocked to the ground, stunned. Rolling over onto his back, Jim's eyes widened in alarm and disbelief as he faced the giant praying mantis. It had followed him!

Jim shook his head clear and reached for his hockey stick, its smooth metal surface dancing with the orange-yellow firelight. The mantis reared up and raised one of its massive front legs to strike.

"*KREEEEEEEEEEEEE!*"

The mantis sliced at Jim but missed as he rolled out of the way and moved closer to one of the immense tree trunks that ringed the circle of the clearing. The mantis struck again, hitting the wet ground with a loud THUNK! Its bladed foreleg was lodged so deeply in the sodden ground the creature could not get it free.

"*KREEEEEEEEEEEEE!*"

Struggling to free its trapped body, the monster swung around and came face to face with the orangutan statue. The mantis raised its other foreleg and scythed the statue's head clean off its shoulders, screeching in frustration and anger.

As the mantis hissed and reared up, Jim ran toward the creature and whacked at its free foreleg with his hockey stick. The mantis screamed at him and knocked him across the clearing. Jim hit the ground hard and struggled to get to his feet as fast as he could. The mantis, its once trapped foreleg now freed, sprang toward Jim. It landed on top of him in seconds, pinning Jim and the duffle bags to the ground with its enormous weight.

"*KREEEEEEEEEEEEEEEEEE!*"

The mantis' head lowered toward Jim's until he and the hideous giant insect were almost eye-to-eye. Its slobbering mandibles dripped onto Jim's face and chest, and he could smell the creature's foul stench. It made him want to vomit.

KLIK KLIK KLIK KLIK!

Everything seemed to move in slow motion, and Jim stared into the creature's chomping jaws, finally defeated. "This can't be it," he said, closing his eyes and waiting for the killing blow.

"*KREEEEEEEEEEEEEEEEEEEEEEEEEEE!*"

With a deafening scream the praying mantis raised its head and prepared to strike.

Thunk! Thunk! Thunk!

When no deathblow came and the creature suddenly went limp and fell off him, Jim dared to open one eye.

"Wha–?!"

Opening both eyes now, Jim saw the moon finally begin to appear from behind scudding black storm clouds. To his right was the hulking mass of the praying mantis, now lying dead on its side, its head filled with several large spears. A smile spread across Jim's lips, and then he saw the silhouette of a lean, tattooed tribesman standing atop the mantis and holding a spear aloft in triumph. Behind him, in the flickering shadows of the fire, Jim could just make out more tribesmen lurking in the near distance, their eyes bright in the moonlight.

"Th-thank you," he muttered. "Who are you?"

The leader hopped off of the dead mantis and walked over to where Jim still lay. The Headhunter's tattooed face remained in an impassive stare for a few seconds as he leaned in close to Jim. *He seems to be studying me,* Jim thought. *But why?*

The Headhunter's face suddenly crinkled into a broad, friendly smile. Jim opened his mouth to ask another question, but his eyes rolled back into his skull and he passed out from exhaustion.

03. Enter the
HEADHUNTERS

It had finally stopped raining, and the moon was shining through blue clouds, casting an eerie light on the jungle. Insects buzzed around the midnight sky like rush hour traffic on a crowded motorway, the air alive with the screams of the cicadas and other nocturnal creatures. Only an hour before, an unnatural tropical storm had lashed the jungle. But now the night was just like any other in Borneo.

Smothered in dense rainforest, Borneo was the third largest island on Earth. It produced much of the oxygen needed for human survival. It was one of nature's last uncharted territories – an adventurer's dream. It was also where Jim and Rufus had been headed when they boarded *The Flying Coffin*, so in a way the unfortunate plane had succeeded in getting them to their destination.

Above all, Borneo was a place of secrets and surprises, and it would prove to be more than a dream for Jim Regent. It would become his biggest – and darkest – nightmare...

✪

Silhouetted against the moon, the scouting party of Iban Headhunters made their way through the jungle, carrying Jim's unconscious body. He was tied to a strong but flexible branch by his wrists and ankles, his body swaying to and fro. The two bags were hung securely around his shoulders, his hockey stick occasionally smacking the jungle floor as the small party wound their way through the foliage.

Jim's special hockey stick was constructed of a lightweight and durable metal by Ruthie's twin brother, Albert, who had been a brilliant scientist before his tragic death two years ago. He had designed the hockey stick to withstand almost any kind of damage, and Jim was amazed at just how tough it seemed. He had taken the hockey stick with him everywhere, and, even after all that had just happened in the past few hours, the stick had barely a scratch on it.

Albert had also made Jim a special watch that he wore every day. It was made of the same metal Albert had used for the hockey stick, and like the stick, it had taken a beating and showed barely any sign of wear. Jim never went anywhere without it, just like the hockey stick and his lucky puck.

The continuous bouncing and banging eventually brought Jim back to consciousness, and he struggled to orientate himself and figure out what was happening.

"Where? What?" His voice was croaky and his throat parched and sore. As the Headhunters turned to look his way, he tried speaking again. "Water?"

After a few seconds of quiet glances between the Headhunters, a water skin was pushed to his lips by a pair of bony hands. Gasping under the steady flow, Jim managed to swallow a few gulps. It was hard to drink hanging the way he was. He sipped some more and grimaced. The water tasted warm, but he was grateful for it nonetheless. His side hurt and the continuous bouncing did not help matters. His crude bandage had been removed and better ones wrapped around his middle.

Jim tried to wriggle out of his bonds, but the closest Headhunter placed his hands over Jim's and shook his head firmly. Jim opened his mouth to respond but the Headhunter shook his head again and increased the grip on Jim's hands. Realizing there was nothing he could do, Jim stopped struggling and let himself be carried up and down vine-covered pathways and around and through twisted jungle roots as his rescuers slowly worked their way up into even denser jungle. The tribesmen travelled in silence, making the whole experience even more surreal for Jim.

Following the party was a small creature that remained hidden in the jungle, only occasionally stopping to part the dense leaves with a small, hairy, orange hand and monitor the Headhunters and their bound guest.

After a little while Jim attempted conversation again, but the only response was to have more water pressed to his lips. Eventually Jim's throat felt better and he found talking easier.

"Hey! Uh… guys?"

There was no response. Jim was starting to worry. The only time he ever saw men carried through the jungle like this was in old movies, and usually those men were prisoners destined for the cooking pot. The thought sent a shiver down his spine.

"Look, not that I'm not, uh, grateful to you guys and everything, but…"

Jim glanced to his side and gulped. He was staring down the side of a steep, rocky incline that fell away into the mist below. The tribesmen did not seem nervous in the least as they continued on their way.

"It was great of you to kill that giant, freakish bug for me and all that. And I appreciate the lift, I really do…"

Jim's thought came to an abrupt end as he realised they had started to cross a very deep ravine using a fallen log as a bridge. Jim closed his eyes and began to whisper the names of his loved ones to distract himself.

After what seemed like forever the little party approached a ramshackle longhouse on stilts that stood on the edge of a fast-flowing river. The sides of the building were intricately decorated with leafy patterns, and a warm, welcoming fire glowed from within. Jim thought the building had to be over two hundred metres long and about that many years old as well.

Passing another totem pole at the entrance to the camp, this one much smaller than the one he saw in the clearing, Jim was carried along a walkway to a veranda overlooking the most spectacular views of the surrounding jungle. Hanging from one of the doorways like a bunch of onions was a cluster of skulls. Jim couldn't tell if they were human, monkey, shrunken or something else just as scary. He shuddered and tugged at his binds.

"Can you please just put me DOWN," he shouted, surprised at the strength and anger in his voice.

Within seconds, long, skeletal fingers were at work swiftly, untying the ropes that bound his hands, and a machete swung with precision to slice through the thick ropes that bound his feet. Jim crashed to the ground with an "OOF!" and lay there for a while, trying to move his achy limbs and get the blood flowing back into his hands and feet.

He could see the mud of the jungle floor several metres below the wooden slats of the walkway he was lying on, and for a moment it seemed as if something was staring back at him. Jim was distracted but looked back at the tribesmen and said, "Thank you".

Before he could stand up, he heard a familiar voice close by in the darkness.

"Jim? Jim, is that you?"

His heart skipped a beat. Jim's tired eyes searched the nearby darkness, hoping against all hope that it was his best friend. "*Rufus?* Rufus McFly, is that you?"

As Rufus moved into the firelight, Jim couldn't help but smile with joy.

"It *is* you! Rufus, I thought you were dead! I have never been happier to see you in my life!"

"You too, Jimbo," said Rufus, as the two friends laughed and gripped each other in a tight hug. Rufus looked as bruised and battered as Jim, and his hair and clothes were a mess – but he was alive!

"What happened after you fell? How did you survive?"

Rufus looked away, seemingly embarrassed. "Well, it was kind of a blur... I happened to land on this enormous plant. It cushioned my fall, but then things took a weird turn – I think it tried to eat me!"

"A flower tried to eat you?"

"It was a *huge* flower," replied Rufus indignantly. "With teeth! Then these guys showed up just in time and rescued me, then brought me here."

"Who are they, Rufus?" whispered Jim. "What are they going to do with us? Are they going to eat us – or shrink our heads?" He was beginning to panic.

"Calm down," replied Rufus. "They're Iban Headhunters. We're in Borneo, Jim! Although I'm not exactly sure *where* in Borneo we are. But the Iban are renowned for their ingenuity and hospitality. I know we'll be treated well."

Just then two Headhunters approached and lifted Jim, carrying his weight without any problem, despite the fact that each tribesman looked quite scrawny and almost fragile. As they carried Jim toward a clearing by the longhouse, he glanced over his shoulder at Rufus, who was walking behind them, a nervous look on his face.

"Uh… are you sure about that, pal?"

04. The Rite of the
ORANGE MOON

Jim soon found himself tied up once more, this time bound to one of the giant totem poles that dotted the clearing near the longhouse. Thick ropes had been wrapped around his chest to stop his limp body from falling. Jim's vest top was shredded and he had a bloody scratch across his chest, his bandages around his middle were soaked with sweat. He must have passed out, delirious and sweating from his injuries. The perimeter of the clearing looked like a forest of totem poles, Rufus could make out the intricate carvings of orangutan heads and what he noted were other Iban motifs. A lot of them were faces with sinister expressions. Beyond them, a mountain rose up out of the midnight blue sky, the mighty Mount Kinabalu. It looked vast and eerie bathed in the glow of the moonlight.

Rufus was not tied up, but the group of Headhunters surrounding him made it clear that he was not much freer than Jim. When some tribesmen started a fire in the middle

27

of the clearing and placed a large pot on top of it, even Rufus got worried that perhaps things were going to get ugly.

As the liquid in the pot boiled away, Jim struggled to see what was in it. "They can't be thinking of boiling us alive and making us their lunch, can they, Rufus? Please tell me that's not what they're doing…"

Before Rufus could answer, a wizened Iban shaman, bandy legged and covered in a cloak of feathers and jewellery made of bones, arrived at the pot and reached into a medicine bag hanging from a leather strap on his waist. With great dexterity, he pulled out strange looking ingredients and dropped them into the bubbling liquid with his long fingers. All Rufus and Jim could do was watch in silent fear.

One by one, elaborately tattooed Headhunters, dressed ceremonially in bright colours and hung with garlands of shrunken heads, appeared from behind each totem pole. They moved slowly in a solemn ritual and shuffled towards the centre of the clearing, creating a circle around Jim.

"Hummanahhummanahhummannahhummanah!" The Headhunters' chant filled the air, and the din of the jungle seemed to recede. Jim and Rufus were petrified, unable to move as they watched events unfold.

The shaman's long, spindly fingers flickered in the moonlight as he worked, sprinkling leaves into the pot, then the tusks of a wild boar, and the pot started to bubble more violently. All Jim and Rufus could focus on were the intense, almost hypnotic eyes of the shaman as he worked, glimpsed through the smoke and steam now coming from the cauldron. The shaman added some bright orange powder from a tiny, intricately carved bone bottle.

As the shaman stirred the bubbling pot with a spoon that looked like it had been carved from a large tusk, a spectral, phosphorescent, orange mist began to swirl from its depths, casting a ghostly glow into the night sky. He reached into the pot with one hand and scooped some of the now luminous and smoking orange liquid into a crude wooden cup, then walked over to where Jim was lashed to the totem pole. The shaman placed one hand on Jim's forehead, and the ice-hockey player fell unconscious.

"Hey, what are you doing to him?" Rufus shouted as he jumped to his feet, but no one answered him. The tribesmen surrounding him drew closer to prevent him from running to help his best friend and made him sit down once more.

The shaman placed the crude cup to Jim's lips and poured the liquid down his throat. Rufus could only watch in helpless terror as the throng of Headhunters became agitated, throwing their hands in the air and rattling their garlands of shrunken heads. Their pupils rolled up into their skulls until only the whites were visible, and their chanting increased.

"Hummanahhummanahhummannahhummanah!"

Several Headhunters fell to their knees all around Jim, their hands extending toward him in supplication. The others danced wildly, twirling bones and machetes in a frenzied celebration as a phantasmagorical orange mist swirled out of the pot and surrounded Jim in an unnatural whirlwind. Clouds streaked across the moon, which had now turned a vibrant shade of orange, as the peak of Mount Kinabalu appeared in silhouette before it.

Jim regained consciousness with a shudder, and tensed when he saw that he was shrouded in an eerie orange mist. All the ceremonially dressed Headhunters were now surrounding Jim in concentric circles, their hands thrust skyward. At the front of the crowd several Headhunters were holding aloft the severed head of the orangutan statue taken from the sacred burial grounds, which now seemed to be floating just above their fingertips.

Back in the midst of the orange storm a transformation was occurring. Jim was changing, his eyes bulging and his features contorting in pain. Jim's right arm expanded and ripped through his shirt, then his left one. His arms were massive, muscled and suddenly covered in a fine orange fur as a distinctive tattoo was now burning itself onto his right bicep. The watch on his left hand popped off his wrist and fell to the ground.

Jim's body continued to contort in pain as it changed

and grew larger. The laces of his boots snapped as large ape-like feet burst from their confines and his legs grew double in thickness, tearing through his trousers. After a few agonising seconds, the orange mist began to dissipate and Jim's transformation was complete.

In the place of his human form stood a gigantic creature covered in thick orange fur: half-man, half-orangutan. The remains of his clothes lay at his feet in tatters, along with the thick ropes that had once bound him. As he struggled to clear his head and make sense of what happened, he saw Rufus looking at him. His friend's mouth was hanging open.

"My god, Jim," whispered Rufus. "What happened to you?"

The shaman and all of the Headhunters present fell to the ground and lay prostrate before Jim.

"What…? What have you *done* to me," cried Jim. "*What AM I?*" He slowly raised his hands to his face, and then looked at the moon, which was still glowing orange in the sky. It seemed to grow brighter as he stared at it, until it cast a halo down from the heavens and around his body, causing Jim to glow. He looked over at Rufus, who was still standing frozen in his place, helpless and horrified. There were tears in Rufus' eyes.

Jim threw back his head and screamed in fury. His wide-open mouth revealed long, sharp, animal fangs.

"*WHAT HAVE YOU DONE TO ME?*" he roared, his voice echoing across the clearing and deep into the jungle.

The shaman rose from the ground and stood before Jim, looking tiny in front of the gigantic creature he had created.

"We have fulfilled your destiny. As Follower of the Orang-eee…"

"My *destiny*," interrupted Jim angrily. "What on earth are you talking about?"

The shaman held up a long, bony hand to silence Jim.

"Yes, your destiny – and ours. Now come! Follow me and I will explain all…"

05. The
PINK PEARL

Inside the longhouse, Jim and Rufus stood quietly in front of the shaman. Jim's knuckles touched the floor as he stared blankly at the man, saying nothing. There was an awkward silence.

"I am Sengalang, Iban shaman, *manang*, headhunter, witch doctor, lah? Call me what you will…" He lifted his staff and slapped his bare feet across the floorboards toward a darkened area of the great room. Then he stopped in his tracks and turned on the spot very slowly, his piercing stare burrowing deep into Jim.

Jim could only stare back silently, still frozen in shock.

Suddenly, there in front of them all was a long wooden wall decorated with swirling patterns. As the shaman stood before it with a big, mysterious grin on his face, the swirling patterns slowly resolved themselves into moving images.

"And so," began Sengalang, "since the dawn of time my people worshipped the Man of the Jungle, the Orangutan, the most powerful of all our gods."

Jim and Rufus could feel themselves drawn in by the shaman's hypnotic voice, mesmerized as the swirling images played out events in Sengalang's story.

"It is spoken of, in ancient prophecy, that one day our protector will walk the earth to save us all. It tells of a white man who will fall from the sky and do battle with the Dragon of the Temburong, taking the form of the Wild Man and leading the Iban people to salvation."

As the shaman spoke, Jim watched as the swirling images replicated the tale of his and Rufus' journey to Borneo. His mouth hung open as he saw an image of the rickety old propeller plane they had boarded only hours before, followed by a blinding lightning bolt that seemed to actually strike the wooden wall, smoulder, then crack and burn the wood. Then the image showed Jim fighting the giant praying mantis and was just as quickly replaced by an image of a small pink orb. The brightness of this tiny sphere was so intense it almost burned itself into Jim's retinas; it was brighter than anything Jim could remember seeing. He brought up a hairy hand to shield his eyes, and the shaman continued with his tale.

"The Pink Pearl rests at the heart of our very culture. It is the source of our creation, lah."

The image of the pink pearl shifted, and Jim and Rufus saw it being grabbed by a shadowy, clawed hand as its light was extinguished. The images on the wall then went dark and disappeared.

"It has been stolen by the Tribe of Shadows," the shaman continued, "and only you can liberate it from their evil grasp."

Sengalang's eyes were burning. Jim finally spoke to break their probing intensity.

"Tribe of Shadows," repeated Jim. "Are you making this stuff up? This is all a joke, right?"

"No, Wild Man! You think I jest? A malevolent force has permeated this land, spreading slowly across the world like a plague. Life is being extinguished by this great evil! The Pink Pearl, our most cherished totem, has been stolen from the sacred place of the dead at the summit of Mount Kinabalu, causing crops to fail and the land to go barren. If the pearl is not recovered soon, the fate of the entire world is uncertain.

"The Pink Pearl is the balance between harmony and devastation, peace and war, yin and yang. In the wrong hands it would become the deadliest of weapons. I would do more myself, but I have been cursed and cannot leave the confines of this clearing. I am the most powerful and ancient of my kind, but I cannot venture beyond until the curse is lifted. Luckily, I have foreseen the oncoming storm and set a plan in motion, a plan that was many years in the making. I have been planting the seeds of our salvation in you, Wild Man! For many years I have been watching you, watching as you have matured into a fine, strong man, as you have slowly been prepared for this special role..."

Sengalang leaned forward, then took Jim's right hand and touched the spider tattoo. "I was the one who gave you this tattoo, Jim Regent. All those years ago in Thailand. You do not remember this, as was my intention. It has special powers, as I am sure you are well aware, lah. But the magic can be tampered with by the Shadow Emperor, who rules the Tribe of Shadows, which is why I accelerated your transformation now. You must become as powerful as possible before setting off to find the Pink Pearl."

The shaman walked over to a dark corner of the room and returned with something hidden beneath a tattered cloth. Sengalang placed the object at Jim's feet, then removed the cloth and revealed an ornate compass set into an ancient ape skull. The shaman leaned in close to Jim again, his face suddenly sinister and threatening.

"The future of the Iban people is at stake, Wild Man. You have no choice in your destiny, lah. You will take this," the shaman said, all softness gone from his wrinkled face. "It will be your guide during the long and perilous journey on which you must now embark."

Carefully, Jim took the skull in his giant hands and studied it up close.

"Why me? I'm just an ice-hockey player..."

Before Jim could protest further, an orange mist seeped out of the skull and took the form of Sengalang's face. Its mouth opened and it spoke in the shaman's voice.

"Your protests are meaningless. The journey begins now! The sacred mist of the Orang-eee will transport you through time and space on your quest to rescue the Pink Pearl from the Shadow Emperor. And when the gods permit, I will offer you guidance through the skull."

Jim and Rufus stared dumbstruck again as the blank wall once more began to swirl with dozens of images: ancient civilizations, cities, monsters and battles, all from long ago and far away. Jim could barely make out what he was seeing, the ghostly images whooshed by so fast: the lost city of the Incas, Machu Picchu; the skyline of Manhattan; the Great Wall of China; the Cambodian temples of Angkor; the snowy peaks of the Himalayas; the feathered Navajo of Monument Valley; the ancient Egyptian pyramids; the rice fields of Vietnam; boiling lava pools and exploding jungle clad volcanoes…

As the images flickered across the wall, both Jim and Rufus became more and more overwhelmed. They wanted to look away but found they couldn't, and soon tears pricked their eyes. This was all too much… *What could two people do to take on all this?* thought Jim.

"The skull has charted an epic quest for you, Wild Man, leading you to strange and exotic locations scattered through time and space. The path will be dangerous, but on this quest you must collect each of the ingredients that make up the Elixir of Life!"

Sengalang's words stopped Jim's thoughts. It was all too much – you must do this, you must do that. Jim snapped himself out of his trance and gathered himself for a second before pointing a massive finger at the shaman. Jim was so angry he was shaking.

"Hang on just a minute! Who are *you* to tell us what we have to do? You say you're... what was your name again?" Jim asked.

"Sengalang," the shaman replied in a calm voice.

"Hang on, Sengalang, I thought I had to find this Pink Pearl thing. What's this Elixir of Life that I'm now supposed to find as well?"

Annoyed, Sengalang pointed a long, spiny finger back at Jim, touching Jim's tip to tip, then pushed his finger away with the smallest of movements. Jim's hand recoiled instantly, leaving him looking surprised – even a little scared.

"Bringing back the Pink Pearl will save the world from total devastation. That is your ultimate destiny. But if you wish to become human again you must also bring back the Elixir." Sengalang stared at Jim, almost daring the young man to challenge his authority again. After several long seconds, Jim sighed and put his head in his hands.

"Why did you have to turn me into an *ape*? Why couldn't

I have done this as a human?"

Sengalang turned and slowly walked away.

"We are *all* apes, Wild Man. You are simply stronger..."
The shaman turned to face Jim and Rufus one last time. He
raised his hand and pointed it at the skull that now lay in
Jim's lap. The skull began to glow bright orange... and
then dimmed again, settling back into a dull
bone-whiteness. "Now, it is time to go. The Orang-eee
grows impatient!"

"Wait a minute," Jim protested. "If I go, Rufus goes as
well. Otherwise, no deal."

Sighing in exasperation, Sengalang approached Rufus and
grabbed his mop of hair between his fingers and tipped the
young man's head sideways. He pushed Rufus' glasses down and
stared deeply into his eyes. Sengalang did not look impressed.

"Why would you wish to have this *orang bodoh* as your
companion?" the shaman snapped. When he saw that Jim
was determined, Sengalang slowly nodded his head.

"Er, what's an *orang*-," began Rufus, but Sengalang cut
him off before he could finish his question.

"Very well," said the shaman. "He will be your servant
on this most sacred of quests. Now go! Take the skull, and
do not lose it or cast it aside, or you will maroon yourself
in a foreign land or time with no chance of returning.
It is your only means of communication with me, and your
only lifeline to our true reality..."

✪

Back outside the longhouse, Jim and Rufus stared blankly at each other. Neither had the words to express their confusion. They began gathering their bags and looked around the clearing.

Headhunters young and old were now going about their business as if nothing special had happened. Some tended the fire, others cooked, and some talked quietly amongst themselves. Aside from the noises of the jungle and the crackle of the fire, the night was peaceful and still.

Jim hefted his duffle bag across his massive shoulders and both he and Rufus stared at the skull. Rufus was holding on to a tuft of fur on Jim's giant forearm, craning to get a better look, when the compass set into the skull's forehead spun wildly and an orange whirlwind enveloped the two friends.

"Aaaaaa–?" cried Jim, as Rufus dug his fingers deeper into Jim's forearm and buried his face in the soft, thick fur.

"I'm gonna be si–" cried Rufus.

"Good luck, Wild Man," was the last thing they heard before the orange whirlwind whipped the world from view.

06. March of the
ANTS

Amidst the swirling orange vortex, Jim and Rufus tumbled around and around, Jim's fur standing out at all angles, one hand clenching the Headhunter Skull close and the other wrapped tightly around Rufus.

"Remain calm, Wild Man," the skull said, echoing all around him.

Rufus was doing the exact opposite as he whimpered into Jim's fur. His body felt like it was being stretched like an elastic band, and his baggy shorts flapped uncontrollably in the intense wind.

After what seemed like an eternity, though it was barely a few seconds, the whirlwind slowed and the orange mist evaporated. The pair crashed to the ground with a thud.

"*OOF!* Where are we *now?*" asked Jim, his head spinning and his eyes adjusting to their new surroundings in the early morning light. As he shook his head clear he began to sense a thickness in the air, charged as if with electricity. He heard a rumble of thunder in the distance, then the croaking of frogs and chirping of insects, then birds flapping and taking flight all over the jungle. Everything seemed more intense – clearer – more lucid. Reality seemed heightened. His hearing was sharper, his vision more acute... Jim felt stronger, more powerful, more dizzy...

"Are you okay, Jim? You have gone a funny shade of ora–"

"Don't be clever Rufus, not now..." Jim glared at Rufus, cutting him off in mid sentence.

"My head is spinning!" sulked Rufus. "Is it me, or does everything seem larger and, well, different?"

"Like me, you mean," Jim responded angrily. "Look at what they've done to me! Why me? What kind of a freak am I now, Rufus?"

"I'm sorry, Jimbo. It's a shock, I know, but we'll figure it out. I think I have heard of this curse of the... what was it called? Werangutan! I'm sure I read about it in a book once when I was researching something in the library. The Iban revere the ape and think of him as their protector."

"That's what Sengalang said, didn't he? But a *werangutan*? What the hell even *IS* a werangutan?" Jim was becoming angrier by the minute.

"I didn't think it was really true," said Rufus. "I thought it was just a legend or some sort of fairy tale..."

"Does this *look* like a fairy tale?" cried Jim. "I can't just turn this on and off, can I? There's nothing made up about this – I'm a giant ape creature! With orange fur! In the middle of a hot and humid *jungle!*"

Rufus put a reassuring hand on his friend's massive arm. "I'm so sorry, Jim. I'm still your best friend. We'll find the Pink Pearl and that elixir Sengalang was rambling on about –"

"No," said Jim, pulling himself together. "First we find Ruthie, that's what we came here to do."

"But Sengalang said –"

"I don't care what that wizened old man told us, Ruthie comes first!" Jim reached into his duffle bag and pulled out the tattered piece of the map Ruthie had sent him, then handed it to Rufus.

"It's definitely from her, Rufus. It has to be. Look at the handwriting, she obviously wrote it in a hurry."

Rufus pushed his glasses higher up on his nose and studied the map closely. On the map was what looked like a mountain nestled at the top of an island, a large "X" placed right over it. *But did 'X' mark the spot?* wondered Rufus. He turned the map to face Jim.

"Well, one thing we definitely know is that it must be Mount Kinabalu," he said, getting more and more excited as he talked. "We were headed toward Kota Kinabalu, the town in the foothills of the mountain, to refuel before travelling on to a tiny village in the Temburong district of Brunei. I made notes in my journal, hold on."

Rufus reached into his bag and pulled out his book and mechanical pencil. He tucked the pencil behind his left ear as he flipped through the journal. "Here, you can see where we were supposed to go on this map I drew. But then we got caught in that storm and lost all sense of direction, and now we're…"

"Lost," finished Jim. "In the middle of nowhere. No, slap *bang* in the middle of nowhere, more like it. I haven't got a clue where we are, and this skull compass thing isn't much help right now. And to top it all off, I've been beaten with the ugly stick and dosed with some weird monkey magic!"

Jim suddenly felt a huge wave of sadness crash over him. Used to being a winner in life and always on top of his game, things had changed once his ankle was injured and he could no longer play ice hockey professionally. Since then he had been searching for something to give his life meaning again. He looked at Rufus and saw his friend staring back at him, Jim realising he had to pull himself together for Rufus' sake – and Ruthie's. He could indulge in self-pity later, when this was all over.

"Well, first thing we need to do is refuel our stomachs," said Rufus calmly. "Food and water will make us feel much better, and then we can make some sort of plan and figure out what to do. Since both Ruthie and Sengalang's mission have Mount Kinabalu in common, we should use that as our starting point."

44

Rufus reached into his duffle bag again and handed a chocolate bar to Jim, then opened one for himself. He popped open the lid of his water bottle and passed it to Jim after taking a big swig. "I bought these bars at that little airport before we left," he said. "Black forest chocolate, or something like that. Have some, they're pretty good. Uh… you do still eat human food, right? Or do you want some bananas?" Rufus couldn't help but smile.

Jim shot Rufus a peeved look, and then fumbled with the bar's wrapping. The chocolate was tiny in his large hands, and he struggled to open it. "It's too difficult with my monster hands!" he grumbled loudly.

Rufus reached over and opened the wrapper for Jim, who then swallowed it in one bite. He then downed all the water in Rufus' bottle in one gulp.

"Jim, we need to ration out suppl… *ouch*!" Rufus looked down to see his outstretched hand covered in tiny red ants. "Ow ow ow ow! These things bite!"

Rufus was now on his feet, shaking his hand wildly, his body moving in a kind of silly dance. Jim could not help but laugh, and it felt good. He realised he had not laughed in quite some time. When Rufus sat back down next to him, Jim reached for his own duffle bag, digging around for his watch. Maybe he could use its compass to figure out where they were. But the watch that once fit snugly around his wrist would now only fit around one of his giant fingers.

"Well, I guess this is better than nothing," he said. Looking at the watch made him think about Ruthie, and he was anxious to get moving again. As the two friends stood and figured out which direction to start off in, they suddenly heard a distant drumming sound that seemed to get louder with each second.

Dum dum dum dum dum dum, like thousands of marching feet.

"What *is* that?" said Jim, trying to use his heightened senses to get a better look.

The trees around them began to shake. After a few seconds they parted in the distance as if a bulldozer had come barrelling through.

Jim's eyes widened. "Rufus... run! *Now!*"

Suddenly an army of gigantic red ants swarmed at Rufus and Jim from all sides, and as the pair ran, burning balls of acid began to sizzle past their ears. Several exploded against the trees as Jim and Rufus ran as fast as they could.

"Since when do ants shoot acid?" shouted Rufus. He didn't even want to think about what else they might be able to do.

Jim grabbed Rufus as if he weighed no more than a feather, and threw his friend over his shoulder. As Rufus clung on to the duffle bag that was also across his shoulders, Jim glanced up and a brilliant idea hit him. He reached into the overhead branches and lifted himself in the air, swinging from branch to branch as quickly as he could.

"Hang on, Rufus!"

As Jim swung higher and higher into the vine-covered trees, the ground started to shrink further away. But the army of giant ants kept coming. Several acid balls zipped past a little too close for comfort as Jim tried to disappear higher into the trees.

Their luck ran out when they came to a clearing and there were no more vines for Jim to hang on to. Spotting a giant overturned tree ahead, Jim did a somersault and landed on it. He still needed to get used to his new body, as he landed a little roughly, nearly knocking Rufus loose and down into the crevasse below.

"Watch it, Jim!" his friend cried, as Jim began to make his way across the makeshift log bridge. He chanced a look behind him and saw the ant army following right on their heels, already making their way onto the log bridge.

"These guys just won't give up!"

Jim had almost made it across the fallen tree when the weight of the ants caused the old, rotting log to give way in an explosion of bugs, wood splinters and dead leaves. The log beneath him fell away, and Jim and Rufus began falling down the deep crevasse.

Thinking quickly, Jim grabbed onto some thick vines that grew on the side, and their trip to a certain death was postponed with an abrupt jolt. Rufus lost his grip and began to fall, but Jim reached out with one of his massive feet and grabbed his friend. He began to swing like a pendulum, gathering speed so they could get high enough in the air to land on the jungle ground above them.

The giant red ants were now cascading into the crevasse by the hundreds, like shiny crimson apples falling from a shaken tree, and Jim felt so relieved he actually began to enjoy his new abilities. Yodelling like Tarzan, he landed nimbly on the ground and Rufus, hanging a metre or so lower, crashed heavily into the cliff edge, spread-eagled in a wall of mud.

"OOOF! Aargh... *Jim...*" Rufus spluttered, the wind shot from his lungs and his face spattered with mud as he started to peel away – and drop!

From nowhere, several skinny but very strong arms darted out and grabbed Rufus from above.

"Wha...?" Was all Rufus could manage as he looked up and into the faces of a baby orangutan and several grey-and-black gibbons.

Jim finally realised what had happened, reached over and lifted Rufus' weight onto more solid ground.

"Oops!" he smiled.

07.

TUAK ATTACK

As Jim and Rufus watched, the young orangutan spoke to them with a series of hoots and whistles, but neither human could understand what was being said. After a few more seconds the orangutan sat cross-legged on the jungle floor like a little ginger Buddha. He put his head in his hands as if he were a disappointed child. Jim concluded that the orangutan was the leader of the group, despite its apparent youth, and after a minute the little orange creature turned to its companions and spoke to them at length. All Jim and Rufus could do was look at each other and shrug their shoulders.

The two gibbons leapt to their feet and became very animated. At first it almost looked as if they were break dancing, and Jim found it hard not to laugh. Rufus looked more bemused than anything, and he was trying to make out what the little gibbons were trying to get across. One of the gibbons suddenly approached Jim and slapped him across the face, then sat down looking aggravated.

"What was that for?" shouted Jim.

Rufus held a hand up to stop Jim from getting angrier. "I think they're trying to tell us something," he said. "Something serious."

"Gee, you think so?" answered Jim sarcastically. "Except I can't speak monkey!"

The orangutan and gibbons chatted some more, then a tiny gibbon finger shot up in the air. Rufus couldn't help but think it looked like the gibbon was playing charades.

"First word," said Rufus, and the little gibbon hopped up and down excitedly. The other gibbon started to prance around, swinging his hips and pushing out his chest.

"Model," said Jim. "Woman?"

The first gibbon hopped up and down, putting a finger on its nose and pointing.

"Woman!"

The gibbon then held up two fingers for 'second word', then pointed at Rufus.

"Me," asked Rufus, then realised his mistake. "Human?"

The second gibbon leapt into the air and somersaulted backward, then proceeded to clap excitedly.

"I think we're getting somewhere, Rufus!"

The next word was proving difficult for the gibbons, who then pounced on Rufus and proceeded to drag him along the jungle floor.

"Hey, watch it! Ouch!" he said, trying to get to his feet.

"I think they want us to follow them," said Jim, finally understanding. His statement was rewarded with more hoots and hollering as the gibbons started dancing around. The dance soon turned into a re-enactment as they tried to explain the situation.

Like a pair of little cowboys, the gibbons pretended to have their hands in imaginary holsters, then turned and walked bandy legged away from Jim and Rufus. They then turned quickly on the spot and pretended to shoot each other using their fingers as guns, as one fell on his back in pretend death throes. He opened one eye looked around to see if anyone was watching, then sprung back into a standing position.

"It sounds like someone is being attacked," said Jim. "Maybe even shot at! And these guys want our help…"

Jumping up and down again and screeching, the gibbons began pulling Rufus along with them as the orangutan waved them deeper into the jungle. Grabbing their bags, Jim slung them across his chest and followed.

✪

It was not long before Jim could tell that danger was right up ahead. Gunshots rang out as the gibbons and the orangutan increased their pace by swinging from tree to tree on vines and lianas that hung from above. Leaping into the air, Jim increased his speed and distance in order to keep up with them.

"Nimble little things aren't they?" shouted Jim to Rufus, but he got no answer other than the sound of his friend huffing and puffing behind him as he struggled to keep up.

Rufus was a sweaty mess. His clothes were stuck to him and his breath heaved in his chest as his heart pounded faster than it had in some time. "Slow down, Jim… this humidity… is killing me," he said between breaths. "You may be some kind of superhero now… but I'm still… just an average… *human*… not adapted to this jungle lark!"

As the gunshots rang louder, the two gibbons stopped in their tracks, and Jim had to leap over them before coming to a stop. The lead gibbon raised his hand to halt the group, then made a few gestures that reminded Jim of something a SWAT team might use. They pointed to Rufus and held up their hands as if to say, "Wait." The other gibbon then jumped onto Rufus and pointed to the undergrowth.

"I think they want you to stay here and hide," said Jim. "I'll go with the orangutan and see what this is all about."

"Fine… by me," panted Rufus. "I'll stay here and guard this… this tree. You guys go on. I'll be… just fine."

Jim and the orangutan crept forward for a better look. As Jim parted some leaves they stepped out onto a muddy road on the edge of a cliff overlooking a truly spectacular view of the jungle. The sunlight sent shafts of light streaking across the rainforest, casting shadows between the mountain peaks, while great swathes of mist lay in the lowlands.

As Jim and the orangutan moved stealthily along the roadway, they turned a sharp corner and saw an overturned delivery truck with the word "Tuak" painted on its side, the truck scratched and scarred from a giant branch that now stuck out from its smashed windscreen. The truck's contents had been dislodged, and pouring out of hundreds of smashed bottles was a sticky white liquid mixing with the mud of the road.

All of a sudden, a slender female arm raised a gun from behind the overturned truck and fired it toward the jungle in front of the vehicle. As the shots rang out, Jim turned to look at the direction in which the bullets were headed.

Daka daka daka! Automatic gunfire pinged off the truck's side, filling it with more bullet holes. Bullets seemed to be flying in all directions, then Jim finally saw the attackers – three men armed with machine guns.

They looked like local bandits in westernised clothing, and Jim didn't think they could be tribesmen of any kind. These guys looked as if they meant business, but their eyes looked vacant – as if no one was home, so to speak. Before he could analyse the attackers any further, another round of gunfire hit the truck's radiator, which burst, filling the air with hot steam.

Without even thinking, Jim used the steam as a diversion and sprung into the fray. He grabbed a large rock from the ground and threw it at one of the attackers, catching him square in the chest. He fell like a bowling pin off the side of the cliff into the jungle below.

One down, thought Jim, as he finally caught sight of the truck's driver. She was a familiar vision of beauty, and with a shock Jim realised who he was looking at.

Ruthie!

Before he could shout her name, Ruthie let rip with another round of gunfire, and it was clear she had not seen Jim moving through all the steam. Grabbing the large branch that had damaged the truck, Jim swung it toward the attackers like a baseball bat and hit one of them dead centre. Before Jim could stop it, the branch also hit the side of the truck with a deafening clang, sending out shockwaves in all directions.

Ruthie grabbed her head and squeezed her eyes shut in pain as the truck rang like a giant bell. Jim wanted to run to her and help. His distraction was a mistake, as the final attacker ran toward them with his machine gun blazing.

Before Jim could react, the little orangutan somersaulted to the back of the truck and like a whirling dervish began flinging the open bottles toward the bandit, who was quickly covered in thick white liquid and flying glass. Trying to keep his momentum, the attacker wound up slipping on the liquid and went flying through the air. Jim sprung across the road with an almighty roar, grabbing the bandit by the feet. He slammed the man back and forth like a frenzied puppy with a rag doll. *Bam Bam Bam!* – then let go. The bandit arced through the air high into the trees and disappeared from sight!

Jim saw Ruthie crawling out from behind the truck, her gun still in her hand, and moved toward her. Rufus and the two gibbons came running around the corner as thunder began to echo across the jungle.

"Great work, Wira," said Ruthie, high-fiving the orangutan. The two gibbons helped her up, and as she dusted herself off, she got her first real look at Jim. She did a double take – then quickly recovered her composure, as if seeing a werangutan were no big deal.

"What are you looking at, monkey boy?" she asked Jim.

Jim found it difficult to speak; he still couldn't believe it really was Ruthie in front of him after all these years. His brain seemed incapable of forming words.

"What news, Wira? Apart from these freaks, any new sightings?" she had a cut-glass accent, dark wavy hair and a wild gleam in her eyes. Just her look was enough to make Jim flustered and turn his knees to jelly, as Ruthie asked the young orangutan while holding her head. She squinted at Rufus as if trying to place who he was, then back at Jim. "Thanks for your help, I appreciate it. Shame I couldn't save the truck; she was a prized possession. Uh, not to sound ungrateful, but who *are* you?"

Jim still couldn't speak, and before Rufus had a chance

to answer a massive crack of thunder shook the ground. A white sheet of rain swept suddenly through the undergrowth towards them. As the group ran for cover, the downpour hit them, and they were soaked to the bone in seconds.

08.

MUDSLIDE!

"**Does it ever stop raining** in this blasted country?" shouted Rufus above the roar of the rain. His glasses had slipped off and were now in his pocket, and his hair was plastered against his face, covering his eyes. Jim's fur was damp and matted as well, and within seconds the muddy road started slipping from beneath them, disintegrating into a river of mud. Thunder boomed and trees began crashing to the ground under the weight of the lashing rain.

"We need to get out of here!" Ruthie screamed as lightning flashed and thunder cracked out of the grey skies. Jim was trying to clear a path into the jungle when he heard it again: the sinister, otherworldly laughter that had rocked *The Flying Coffin*. It echoed on the wind for a second and then was gone.

"Did you hear that?" he asked Rufus.

"Hear *what*?" his friend replied.

Another clap of thunder shook the air, as the ground

beneath the group fell away and knocked them to their knees. The orangutan and gibbons leapt high into the trees for cover, as Ruthie, Rufus, and Jim began sliding toward the overturned truck. They hit the side of it with a bang, and the truck began to move closer to the edge of the cliff. Jim braced himself as he grabbed Ruthie to prevent her from falling over the side.

Jim and Ruthie could not help but follow the torrent over the edge and were sent tumbling down the steep slope where the road had once been. Jim held Ruthie with all his strength as the two were swept down the slope, bashing and battering against tree stumps and sharp rocks on the way down the mountainside.

Rufus tried to spot the others through the blinding rain, but without his glasses on he couldn't see much. The road had become a river, and he was soon following the others into the waterfall of mud, screaming Jim's name over the rush of dark slime and boom of thunder.

The trio plummeted through giant leaves and spiky plants on a carpet of rushing water, twisting and turning as they tried not to choke and drown. After a few terrifying seconds the slope came to an end right above a thick, churning lagoon.

With a scream, Ruthie landed first, coming to an abrupt stop as she splashed down on her backside. Jim followed close behind her. Ruthie thought he looked like a chocolate covered orange as he slid down the slope and almost wanted to smile – but she was quickly covered in muddy water herself when Jim landed with a giant splash. As she wiped the mud from her face she saw Jim laughing at her. Her amusement quickly turned to anger and she pushed Jim away. She opened her mouth to say something, but stopped when she heard a crashing high above their heads. She looked up to see Rufus skimming toward them, her truck right behind him.

"*TRUUUUUUUUUCK!*" Rufus screamed at the top of his lungs, before splashing head first into the rapidly filling lagoon.

Thinking fast, Jim grabbed Ruthie and covered her with a giant bear hug. The truck bounced off of Jim and exploded in a fireball. There soon followed a rainstorm of shattered glass bottles and milky white Tuak.

Ruthie and Jim were not hurt, but he was winded by the force of the falling truck. The rain continued to pour, and Ruthie could not even see the roadway far above them. She watched Jim grimace as he pulled a shard of glass from his side, then saw Rufus bob up from the muddy water, coughing and blinded by his own lank quiff.

"That," spluttered Rufus, "was *not* my idea of fun!"

09. Journey to
KAMPONG AYER

"Who the hell are you guys?" asked Ruthie in exasperation. "You certainly know how to show a girl a good time!" She scraped her hair back from her face as the rain continued to pour.

"It's *me*, Ruthie – Jim! Jim Regent!" Admittedly Jim did not expect her to recognise his face since his transformation. But he hoped that she would at least recognise his voice.

"Bull!" was her response.

Jim fished into his waterlogged duffle bag and pulled out a waterproof zipper and handed it to her. Ruthie opened it – inside was the fragment of map that she had sent to her friend.

"How did you get this?" she asked, looking more and more confused.

"It's me – Jim!" he exclaimed, losing his patience. "You sent it to me! That's why we came all this way to find you!"

Ruthie studied Jim for a few long seconds, then stuffed the torn map into a side pocket on her trousers. "We'll talk about this as soon as we get to my place."

Thunder rolled overhead and a fork of lightning struck a tree not more than fifty metres away from where the trio stood in the rapidly filling lagoon. It split the trunk and sent wood shards flying into the electrified air. The rain was so heavy that it made seeing more than a few metres ahead almost impossible, and all three were caked in mud and grime.

"Enough of the spa treatment boys... we *need* to find shelter and get back to a warm fire before we all catch pneumonia!" Ruthie cupped her hands to her mouth and began hooting loudly. Within seconds Wira and the two gibbons swung down from the trees above and joined the others by the lagoon. Within minutes the group had gathered their soaked, muddy bags and Ruthie led them away from the lagoon and deep into the jungle. The rainforest here seemed darker and more menacing, and Jim couldn't shake the feeling that they were journeying into some kind of underworld.

"What's going on in this place?" he asked Ruthie. "Giant insects, mindless bandits, super-storms... You can't tell me any of this is normal!"

Ruthie didn't answer his question, or even turn to look at him. "Cut the chatter boys, we'll have time to talk later. Keep your eyes forward and pay attention!"

When did she get all badass? thought Jim. He had known Ruthie since they were both kids, and she had never been as hard and determined as this. He decided to take her advice and check on how his friend was doing. Rufus looked miserable as he struggled to keep his hair out of his eyes and pick his way through the morass of plant-life without his glasses. Until the rain eased off, his glasses were useless.

Ruthie continued to hack away at the jungle growth, carving a trail for them with skill and precision. As they trudged on the rain started to subside and the insects returned. Rufus was grateful to be able to put his glasses back on, but the tiny buzzing predators made their journey even more unpleasant.

After what seemed like hours, the group finally approached a clearing and stopped by the banks of a fast flowing river. The dark green water, which reflected the trees and sky above, was cool and inviting after the heat and humidity of the jungle. Removing his duffle bag, Jim ran toward the river and dived in with a massive splash. Rufus didn't need convincing: he waded into the soothing rapids, glad of the chance to wash off all the mud this jungle had thrown at him over the past day or so.

Ruthie put her pack down on the riverbank next to an old longboat. She tied her hair back, removed her boots, emptied her pockets and dived into the water like an Olympic athlete. Jim watched her as she burst from the water, flicking her hair back and spraying water in a neat arc across her back. One by one all the gibbons somersaulted into the water, followed by Wira, and soon all of them were clean of grime and feeling a little better.

After ten minutes or so, Rufus and Ruthie climbed out of the river and began putting their boots back on. Jim jumped ashore then shook his great mane of hair, spraying droplets everywhere.

"Okay, okay, enough already," shouted Ruthie, and shot Rufus an evil glare when she noticed him laughing. "You two ready?"

They loaded their packs into the longboat, and Ruthie lowered the propeller into the water. Standing above the engine, she pulled the starter cord and the engine roared to life. The red boat started to move, its engine choking out a plume of black smoke, and then it jerked forward, knocking Rufus off his feet and almost back into the water – until Jim caught him with a huge furry hand.

"Ready?" Ruthie asked with a smirk, then the engine roared like a pack of wild animals and created a plume of spray as the boat shot down the river. Scared that his enormous bulk would cause the boat to pull a wheelie, Jim shifted his weight about as they ploughed on.

Before long they had torn up the rapids and were approaching the mouth of the river. They passed monkeys swinging in the mangrove swamps and tall trees with tentacle-like roots that sank deep into the emerald green water. Rufus pointed at a pair of proboscis monkeys that were swimming in the river and smiled with fascination.

"I've never seen monkeys swimming like that before!"

They flew past stilt houses and fishing villages made of ancient bamboo, eventually making their way into the open waters of the South China Sea. The waters were choppy but the boat crossed them in no time at all, and they arrived at a vast floating village as the sun was setting.

Jim stared at the village, which was made up of hundreds of run down shacks grouped together and mounted on stilts above the water. Tiny, rickety boats were tied to wooden pontoons that led up dilapidated makeshift ladders through holes in the boardwalk. This was Kampong Ayer, a freewheeling, anarchic community, a hodgepodge of old traditions and new technologies, where wood and tin combined to create a shanty village with the atmosphere of an American wild west town.

"Right, boys, here we are," Ruthie said. She reached into the back of the boat and threw a large, stained canvas over Jim.

"Uh, what was that for?" asked Jim, then realised immediately. "I guess the locals may find an eight foot tall walking, talking orangutan a bit strange…"

Ruthie shushed Jim, then waved her hands in a sort of complicated sign language at the gibbons, who quickly darted up into the rooftops.

Jim wrapped himself up as best he could in the canvas

tarp as Rufus gathered their bits from the longboat. Wira exited the boat and peeked around the nearest corner, then waved the group forward.

"Right, coast is clear. Let's move it, fellas," said Ruthie.

Trying to be as inconspicuous as possible, Jim, followed close behind by Rufus, made his way through the village, grateful for the long, wide shadows cast by the setting sun. The walkways glowed an eerie green, and Rufus realised the light was coming from jars filled with fireflies. He crouched down in front of one of the jars to get a closer look and found himself enchanted by their simple ingenuity. He was soon brought back to reality at the sound of the wooden planks creaking and groaning under Jim's great weight. Luckily for the group, the noise of frogs, crickets and other night creatures helped to drown out any noise they made.

From out of nowhere, two little children dressed in tattered clothes and with bare feet burst onto the walkway. Oblivious to the group, they were chasing a large dragonfly. More children peered out of windows and from behind wooden barrels half hidden by rows and rows of drying clothes. One small boy stopped and stared at Rufus, who gave the boy a goofy smile. The boy smiled back, and darted away into the darkness of his hut.

It was a ramshackle place, teeming with colourful characters and animals left to peck and scratch about for scraps of food. An old man, rich with golden teeth, was sitting cross-legged in the shadows chewing on his betel nut. He spat then took a long drag from his pipe, blowing thick blue smoke rings into the humid air. Jim glanced across as the glow from the end of his pipe lit up his weathered face and strangely yellowing eyes, which then faded back into the darkness. The man's thoughts seemed to be elsewhere. He completely ignored the odd-looking group skulking their way through the shadows.

Directly ahead of them stood a large wooden building constructed around an old American caravan made of shiny metal. It was bound together by a spider's web of vines, which grew from its roof and connected the building to the distant tree canopy. The two gibbons grabbed onto the vines and zip-wired along them. At the last minute they somersaulted, dodging aerials and satellite dishes crudely welded to the roof, then dropped into the shadows, disappearing from sight. They were followed closely by Wira, who also slid down the vine and through a trapdoor that opened in the roof.

"Clever," said Rufus, as Jim pointed to a crudely painted, weather-beaten sign with the carved head of a grumpy looking water buffalo at its centre. Below the buffalo were three words: *The Moody Cow*. The sign swung and creaked on its rusty hinges, nudged by the gentle night breeze, and fireflies flashed like flickering neon in a pair of empty beer bottles tied to the signpost.

Jim turned to Ruthie as she pushed him into a narrow, dark alleyway that dipped beneath *The Moody Cow*, down a flight of creaky stairs past a sleepy black dog, which stirred as they slunk past. Its yellowish stare followed their every move in the darkness. Jim's bulk barely fitted along the tight alleyway as Ruthie led him on. He heard a tearing sound from behind. Jim turned and saw that he had caught his tarp on a rusty drainpipe. As he tried to pull it free, Ruthie pushed him forwards. Without warning, the floor dropped away and he fell into darkness.

10. The

MOODY COW

A **light flickered on overhead** as Jim slowly came to his senses. A single bare bulb illuminated a wood-lined cellar, tiny flies buzzing around its halo. The room was lined with what Jim recognised as bottles of Tuak – the white, milky liquid Ruthie had been transporting in her truck. These bottles were labelled with old-fashioned stickers reading 'Moody Cow Tuak'.

Jim jumped as he glanced around and saw Ruthie looming over him. Rufus and Wira lurked behind her in the shadows. They were standing in front of a rusty metal door.

"Okay, no more lies," Ruthie said. "Who are you – really?"

"Ruthie, it's *me* – Jim Regent! I got turned into this… this creature by Iban Headhunters. Ask Rufus, he'll tell you. He saw it all happen!"

"It's true," Rufus nodded, but Ruthie held up her hand to silence him.

"I need proof," Ruthie continued, "and not just this map. You could have stolen that from Jim."

Jim sighed and dug into his duffle bag, pulling out his hockey stick and puck. "Look," he said, pushing them toward her. "You know these are mine. I never travel anywhere without them!"

Ruthie hesitated for a second then scowled at Jim. "Again, you could have stolen them."

Frustrated, Jim grabbed Ruthie's hand and traced the scar that ran across his left eye with her finger. "Don't you recognise this at least? You gave me this scar when you hit me in the face with my lucky puck! It's me, Ruthie. I promise!"

There was a heavy silence. Then Ruthie's face melted into a small smile as tears filled her eyes. "Jim? Is it really you? What happened?"

"It's really me, Ruthie." Jim pulled his face away in embarrassment; afraid he would start crying as well. He and Rufus told Ruthie what had happened since their catastrophic landing in Borneo, and when they got to the end of the tale, Ruthie remained quiet. "So," Jim asked," what do you think?"

Ruthie's eyes flickered, and before Jim could do anything she went limp and fainted, falling into a rack of old bottles that caused a plume of dust to fill the air.

"Well, that went well!" quipped Rufus, as Jim gently picked Ruthie up from the dusty floor. A team of five gibbons soon joined them, and Wira waddled over to a keypad next to the door. He entered the code 1-2-1-0-9-8 and the door creaked open. Wira stepped inside, then reappeared a moment later signalling them to follow. Jim and Rufus looked at each other in bewilderment.

As the ceiling was low, Jim had to duck down until he was almost crawling on all fours, taking care not to drop Ruthie. Once he and Rufus were inside, the door clanged shut behind them, the sound of sliding bolts and locks filling the air. Now they were in total darkness.

Wira flicked some switches and the large room was suddenly aglow with light and noise. Both Jim and Rufus could not believe what they were seeing. The vault-like chamber was filled with recording devices, view-screens and machines spewing ribbons of ticker tape. An old projector with two fuzzy red microphones sat on a shelf in the corner of the room, flickering and clattering with old music videos of Dean Martin and Frank Sinatra. Two large fans on the ceiling whirred steadily, circulating the air within the room, which was far more comfortable than the oppressive heat and humidity outside. The more Jim looked around the more he noticed how dated the technology was. There were pieces of paper pinned to the walls, which were lined with cardboard egg-cartons in an ingenious attempt at soundproofing.

A closer examination of the walls revealed photographs and crude sketches of strange creatures, including one that resembled the giant praying mantis, and a number of smudgy, shadowy creatures of an uncertain nature. Ruthie had obviously been keeping a record of all the strange supernatural phenomena that had been plaguing Borneo. Silently, a realisation began to dawn on Rufus and Jim: Sengalang's story was true, or at least rooted in truth. There was evil at work on the island.

Before Jim could ask any questions, one of the gibbons opened a locked cabinet to reveal dozens of glass vials in every colour of the rainbow. They were labelled with tiny hand-written stickers, all yellowing with age. Rufus and Jim peered at the labels: 'Anti-Venom'; 'Batwing Essence'; 'Spider Bite'; 'Flesh-rot Reviver'; 'Sleeping Dust'; 'Bottled Cicada Scream'; 'Durian Essence' and, finally, a vial that was selected by the gibbon, 'Elephant Pee – Handle With Care!' The gibbon opened the vial and Rufus was instantly hit by a wave of nausea, his eyes watering in pain. Moving away blindly, he banged into a recording device, knocking a roll of tape from its spool. Ribbons of tape shot around the room like silly string as Wira grabbed Rufus and sat him down on a nearby chair. Rufus' face turned red with embarrassment as he brushed his thick mop of hair out of his eyes for the hundredth time.

The gibbon held the tiny bottle under the unconscious Ruthie's nose. Her eyes fluttered open as she inhaled the ammonia smell of the elephant urine, and before long

Ruthie was sitting up and coughing. She blinked and saw Jim and Rufus staring at her intently.

"Wha… What are you two doing in here?" she asked, annoyed. "You shouldn't be in here!"

"What *is* this place?" asked Jim. "It's like spy central down here!"

Ruthie shot Wira a furious look. Then she sighed and her expression softened. She didn't have the strength to be angry right now.

Rufus pushed his glasses further up on his nose, and began pointing at things on the wall. "There's radio transceiver equipment, reconnaissance maps, Top Secret files, newspaper articles from something called *Screams of the Six O'Clock Cicada*…"

Ruthie nodded toward a large, ancient printing press in the corner as Jim helped her to her feet. She led them to the darkened area of the room and then flicked a switch on the printing press. As it came screeching and bleeping to life, a screen flickered on and the latest edition of the newspaper was revealed. Ruthie turned to them and squared her shoulders.

"Since you both were *honest* with me, I can only return the favour. Five years ago I came to Borneo with my brother Albert, and we set up house here in Kampong Ayer. For the first two years it was bliss as we got to know the locals and explore." Ruthie's eyes misted over as she remembered.

"We soon became the heart and soul of this small community when we started making Tuak, a local beverage. I brewed it by myself and was making a nice profit."

"But what's with all the equipment?" asked Jim.

"For the past few years I've trained these gibbons," said Ruthie, pointing to the seven gibbons, who were now lined up in a neat row. "Cute, aren't they? Just don't get on the wrong side of them, trust me. From left to right we have Tingkar, Tiger, Ringgit, Milo and Peng, and our two communications officers who keep the place running, Maggi and Noodle."

Rufus waved at them. Each of them saluted back, making him smile.

"Last but not least is my right hand man, Wira," continued Ruthie, putting her arm around the orangutan. "This little hero keeps the guys in check and coordinates their every move, keeping their eyes and ears open on all the comings and goings in this area. They use the vines to get around and to carry messages from one town to the next. They go everywhere, see everything, hear everything… and inconspicuously. Who, after all, would suspect a monkey in a tree?"

"So are you a newspaper reporter then?" asked Rufus. "Or some sort of spy? Or *both*?" He picked up a document watermarked with the word 'Shadowlab'.

It was stamped TOP SECRET.

Ruthie looked concerned. "I was hired by the British government's intelligence agency to keep an eye on the shadowy goings-on in Borneo. I set up my headquarters here under this guesthouse that Albert and I opened."

"But how can we be in the basement of a building that's built on stilts in a river estuary?" asked Rufus, confused.

"Well, that would be telling," said Ruthie with a sly grin. "Technological research in this area went through the roof once Albert found some private funding for his Dark Matter research station. I still have no idea who built the Shadowlab deep under Mount Kinabalu, but whoever created the lab created this bunker in the bedrock under Kampong Ayer. As long as the shielding is running no one will know it's here and the bunker will remain uncompromised."

Rufus' eyes were wide with excitement. He looked like a kid at Christmas. "You mean there are bigger, more technologically advanced events happening here in the middle of the jungle?"

"Not *in* the jungle," Ruthie corrected. "*Under!*"

Rufus was stunned and speechless, his brain whirring and spinning with questions and thoughts.

Ruthie continued. "Since I've been here the Gibbon Spy Network, or GSN, led by myself and Wira, have been monitoring the increasing Dark Matter power spikes in the area. We hide behind the umbrella of our little newspaper, which as you saw is called the *Screams of the Six O'Clock Cicada*."

"Uh, why that name?" asked Jim intrigued.

"At six every evening the insects and cicadas start their infernal cacophony of noise long into the night. We think this is due to the changes in air pressure caused by the activation of a giant power source under the mountain. We can't be certain, but more and more… 'creatures' have been appearing, and indigenous wildlife has been mutating into monstrous, brainless beasts that are radically changing the natural environment."

"Like the ants and those zombie bandits," said Rufus. He walked over to the carton-lined wall that was covered with images and clippings. All of them were linked by a spider's web of red string, and at the heart of the web was a black-and-white photograph of Mount Kinabalu.

"The paper is the perfect cover for our investigations into the abnormal events that are spreading through Borneo like a disease," continued Ruthie.

Jim was in shock; he couldn't believe his one-time childhood friend was now a spy-cum-paranormal investigator. No wonder she hadn't found his appearance strange!

Rufus continued to flick through the images on the wall and soon spotted a photograph of a little propeller plane being struck by lightning. It was the plane he and Jim had taken to Borneo, *The Flying Coffin*. The picture must have been taken right before the crash. It was out of focus, but Rufus could just make out the nameplate on the front of the plane's nose cone. "Jim! Come and look at this…"

Jim stood next to Rufus and the pair stared at the image. Then Jim saw another photograph, a blurry snap of a giant roaring beast covered in thick red fur. It was *him*! He turned to look angrily at Ruthie, his eyebrows furrowed and confused.

"That's *me*! How could you possibly have taken this?"

"I told you," said Ruthie, crossing her arms across her chest. "We are an intelligence agency. We have spies everywhere, and we aim to know what's going on all over this *unusual* island."

11. *The*

WAITING DARKNESS

Beneath the rainforest, burrowed deep into the earth, a man moved swiftly in the darkness. He was breathing deeply and his heavy, limping footsteps clanged on the metallic floor. His body was swathed in a long, dark cloak, and only a red LED light was visible beneath the cowl. In his hands he carried a flimsy-plast screen illuminated with symbols and a newspaper report of a man tied to a totem pole surrounded by an orange mist.

After a few seconds he arrived at a shielded door, then lowered his face in front of a retina scanner that was embedded in the wall. A beam of blue light lanced out of the shadows and scanned the man's eyeball.

Ping!

The door hissed open and light poured into the dark corridor, illuminating a stencilled sign on the wall: *298*. The man entered swiftly, and the door closed behind him.

The metal room was cold and cavernous. The man's breath was visible and mingled with the white mist that was pumping from tiny grilles near the floor. The room looked like it had seen better days, with view-screens lying at angles, toppled from their mounts; the once shiny metal walls were coated in a thin layer of carbon, and there were cracks in the floor and ceiling where giant black roots had broken through. Everything else in the room look charred and twisted, darkened by what seemed to be the aftermath of an explosion. As the man made his way through the debris he remained intent on the data pad he carried, and became more and more agitated with each passing moment.

"What is it, Gilaaa?" came a deep, raspy voice from an unseen chamber ahead. The man turned a corner past blackened computer screens into an area covered with roots and vines, lit by a large, glowing, spherical machine. At the heart of the machine was a swirling portal, and around the circumference were hundreds of wires and glass vials filled with thick, black, bubbling slime. The machine was fed by tubes that snaked from several vats, some filled with the same dark goo, others filled with vibrant green and pink viscous liquids that bubbled like enormous lava lamps. The tree roots seemed to be drawn to the vats; their tendrils had pierced the glass and were feeding on the dark liquid.

"Doctor Gila," the voice boomed more insistently, "what news have you, my deranged geniussss?"

Doctor Gila finally looked up from his pad and faced the machine. There in the central portal, glowing with malice and pulsating with evil, was a face. It had cold, slitted eyes and a scaled muzzle, and every few seconds a sharp tongue flicked out from a mouth that was lined with serrated fangs. He raised the pad in front of his face and began to read aloud to the creature.

"Man or Beast? Curse of the Werangutan," he began. "Several reports of the so-called 'Werangutan of Kinabalu' came from the Iban Headhunter region, where many have claimed that the appearance of the 'Wild Man' – described as eight feet tall with enormous fangs and a funky haircut – has something to do with the rising of the orange moon, a phenomenon astronomers have always explained as the warping of sunlight in cloud belts across Earth's upper atmosphere…" Doctor Gila paused to clear his throat. "However, experts in Headhunter history claim that the orange moon is directly connected to the summoning of a Protector spirit, which can take the form of a half-man, half-beast hybrid. The orange moon has been viewed as a portent of doom all over the world since–"

"Enough, Gila! Do you think this isss the *one*?" asked the creature.

"I do believe this could be a new Protector, my Lord. He may be the missing link in our research…"

"Darkness is coming, Gila. Double your efforts to capture this beast; I need to know his sssssecret. Time is running out. The Great Storm will soon arrive and this

Dark Matter Scope will release me from my prison," hissed the monster. "Unleash my Tribe of Shadows!"

"Yes, my Lord!" Doctor Gila bowed and left the creature to its thoughts. His black cloak billowed behind him, dragging through the mist that swamped the ground. One by one, black shapes detached themselves from the gloom and lined up behind the doctor, who picked up a strange ornately carved weapon, resembling a cross between a spear and a gun, from a vast array of technologically advanced weaponry. He was ready to command the Tribe of Shadows, personal army of the entity known as the Shadow Emperor.

12. A Hot and
SPICY PLAN

"There you go, monkey boy," said Ruthie as she passed two full bowls filled with hot chicken noodle curry over to Jim. "This should fill you up!"

Before Ruthie could give him a spoon, Jim had buried his face in the thick curry and slurped it up greedily. He hadn't realised how starved he was. It had been days since he and Rufus had last eaten!

"Nice manners, Mister Regent," said Ruthie, laughing and shaking her head. Rufus was also devouring the curry. The heat of the dish was making him sweat, but he was so hungry he didn't care.

"We need to have our wits about us and our bellies full if we want to get into the Shadowlab," said Ruthie, wiping sweat from her brow and putting down her bowl. "There's nothing worse than being ill-prepared for a mission."

"I agree," said Rufus, taking a long drink from his glass of water, followed by a guzzle of the fizzy sarsaparilla drink Ruthie said was a favourite of the locals. As he pushed back his damp hair he let out a small burp. "Pardon me," he said, red with embarrassment.

Ruthie laughed. "Is that the best you can do?"

Deciding to take up the challenge, Jim reached over the table for an unopened can of sarsaparilla, knocking over his water and dragging his massive arm in the remains of his curry. He stared at the can for a few seconds, debating how he was going to open it – the ring pull was too small for his large fingers. Then a smile spread over his face as he gently squeezed the can until it burst. He poured the sweet fizzy liquid into his mouth, spilling some all over his muzzle.

"Geez, Jim, you're an animal," said Rufus. "Am I going to have to train you to eat like a human again when this is all over?"

In response to Rufus' question, Jim let out the loudest, most unnatural-sounding burp any of them had ever heard. One of the gibbons put his hands over his eyes, while another slapped a hand over his mouth. A third sitting high on a stool reached up and grabbed a pair of ear defenders hanging from a nail on the wall and covered her ears, traumatised by the echoing sound. All Rufus and Ruthie could do was laugh hysterically, and soon Jim joined them.

After a few minutes the silliness calmed and the group finished eating. It had been a much-needed release for all of them. The trio was preparing for the long trek into the jungle, on a mission to find the abandoned entrance to the elusive Shadowlab.

Now it was time to plan.

Ruthie cleared the plates and spread out some old yellowing army maps, which were riddled with coloured contour lines and notes. She was trying to pinpoint the grid coordinates her brother Albert had given to her before he disappeared.

"I knew I should have taken him up on his offer to visit the lab when he was working there," said Ruthie. "It would make this so much easier…"

Jim and Rufus began packing their bags with full water bottles, torches, Swiss army knives and other travelling tools. When Jim reached for the Headhunter Skull, Ruthie's eyes widened.

"What *is* that?" she asked.

"What?" replied Jim.

"This," said Ruthie, reaching for the skull.

"No!" shouted Jim. "Don't touch that!"

"Sorry, sorry! Where did you even get it?"

"It was given to me by the Iban shaman. It apparently has the power to help us destroy the darkness and guide us on our quest," Jim said.

"Your quest?" asked Ruthie, confused.

"Yes," added Rufus. "Something about an elixir and travelling to someplace dark and hidden…"

"Well, keep it safe then," she said, stealing one last glance at the macabre object before returning her attention to the maps.

"Don't worry," muttered Jim. "I plan to."

As Ruthie began to fill her backpack, the metal door hissed open and Milo and Peng swung, chattering, into the bunker. Ruthie made some hand signals back at them. Both stood stiffly to attention and then darted through trapdoors on either side of the room.

"Uh… what was that?" asked Jim.

"I've told them to go ahead to a specific grid coordinate and scout out the jungle," Ruthie replied, zipping closed her backpack. "Right, boys, it's time to get going. The old Shadowlab entrance is supposed to be on the north side of Mount Kinabalu."

As Rufus went to grab his duffle bag his hair fell into his face again, and he pushed it back with a sigh. Ruthie reached into a desk drawer and pulled out a pair of scissors.

"First things first," she said. "Before we go anywhere I'm cutting that damn hair of yours!"

✪

Once again Jim was wrapped in a large utility blanket and smuggled through Kampong Ayer, this time down to a floating jetty. Alongside the jetty was berthed a black longboat, sleeker and more technologically advanced than the old red one they had arrived in. Along its side was painted the name *The Black Shadow*.

"Wow, where did you get this beauty from?" asked Rufus, who went to flick his quiff out of his eyes, only to realise that it wasn't there anymore.

"It was the last thing Albert gave to me before he vanished," said Ruthie. "It was his personal transport to and from the Shadowlab. It's equipped for high speeds, and, luckily for Jim, it's modified with stealth mode and advanced stabilisation. We shouldn't have a problem evading prying eyes in this baby."

As they all found their seats, Wira took the controls. Firing up the engines, the orangutan steered the boat out from under the shadow of *The Moody Cow*. Shafts of light pierced the slatted walkway from above, strobing across the excited faces of the little group as they set out on their adventure.

Ruthie leaned over and flicked a switch on the dashboard labelled 'Stealth Mode' and took over from Wira at the helm. "Right, let's go!"

Before any of them could take a breath the boat blasted into the main stream of the river. Rufus' mouth fell open in amazement – and he immediately started choking on a large fly!

"That will teach you to keep your mouth shut!" laughed Jim, slapping his friend across the back with his large tattooed palm. Rufus gasped for air and then, reluctantly, swallowed.

As *The Black Shadow* sped through the tributaries of the river, invisible thanks to its stealth shield, Jim and Rufus caught blurred snapshots of life on the water. Little children frolicked by the banks while their mothers washed and hung colourful laundry. Some of the more adventurous kids swung from overhanging branches and splashed into the green water.

Ruthie steered the boat expertly through rocks and fallen trees as if she were on an Olympics slalom course. It was only as they passed close to a fisherman standing in a rickety old boat that things got a little hairy. As they zoomed past, the fisherman cast his net, and it became caught on the tip of the *The Black Shadow*, making the stealth shield crackle and momentarily fade. The old man briefly locked eyes with Jim. He cried out in shock as he fell out of his boat.

"Gila! Gila! Crazy!" the man shouted as he trod water.

"Oops, that was close!" shouted Ruthie as the shield reasserted itself, cloaking the speedboat from view once more.

✪

After about half an hour the boat entered darker waters. Giant trees with huge buttress roots and fins rocketed into the tree canopy hundreds of metres above.

"I've never seen the jungle like this," said Ruthie, slowing the boat down. "It's almost like the trees are growing… dark."

"I take it that's bad," said Rufus, looking around in awe.

"Yes. *Very* bad," replied Ruthie as she steered the boat to the riverside and shut down the engine. "Right, by my calculations we've gotten as far as we can by river. We'll have to go the rest of the way on foot. Think you boys are ready for a hard slog?"

Jim leapt out of the boat and pulled it the rest of the way to the shoreline, then tied it to a twisted tree root. "What are we wasting time for?" he asked, answering Ruthie's question with another of his own.

Rufus and Ruthie grabbed their bags as Jim slung his over his shoulder, along with a large, coiled line of rope. He checked to make sure his hockey stick was secure, giving it an affectionate pat. "You're coming with me," he whispered. "I have a feeling you'll come in very handy."

Ruthie pulled on her backpack, then strapped two pistols in holsters to her hips, tossing a third to Rufus. Grabbing a large machete from the back of the boat, she put on her sunglasses and turned to the two men.

"So boys… Ready for some action?"

13. Welcome to the
JUNGLE

The going was slow through the unnaturally dense, mutated jungle. The usual dipterocarp trees had warped into monstrous titans reaching skyward like gnarled fingers. The buttress fins were blackened and leathery. The jungle had also become more humid; the air was thick as soup, making it harder for the group to breathe. Ruthie led the way, slicing through leaves and undergrowth with her machete. As usual, Rufus was straggling behind, winded and out of breath.

"If we're heading uphill like we should be, the entrance is that way." said Jim, checking the digital compass that was built into his watch face. The needle was spinning back and forth. "Something's causing distortions in the magnetic fields."

Ruthie glanced at the compass and shook her head. "It must be coming from something hidden deep beneath the jungle. Look around – none of this is normal. All readings are way off the charts. I'm worried it has something to do with Albert."

"What was he doing, exactly?" asked Rufus, coming up behind them. "Those experiments?"

"I'm not absolutely sure," Ruthie replied sadly. "Albert became more distant as his work progressed. Once we'd set up *The Moody Cow* he started going to the Shadowlab for days on end, but he never discussed what he was doing with me. Whenever I asked him he would change the subject or tell me to mind my own business. When the British government contacted me on our long-range scanners, almost two years ago now, I knew something was *very* wrong."

"When was the last time you saw your brother?" asked Jim, hoping the answer would not be too painful for Ruthie.

"The night of the explosion," she replied.

Rufus' eyes went wide. "Explosion?"

"Yes. Last year a huge blast rocked the mountain and destroyed one of its peaks. Albert was at the Shadowlab, and I never saw him again…" Ruthie broke off suddenly unable to speak, took a deep breath and turned her back.

Jim put a giant arm around Ruthie and hugged her, nudging her onward. "Come on, the sooner we get there the sooner we can get some answers."

Ruthie wiped away a few tears and nodded.

As they trekked deeper and deeper into the jungle, the terrain became more and more twisted and perilous.

Every surface was blanketed in slick moss and wet, green vegetation, making the environment slippery underfoot and near impossible to climb.

The only one who seemed to be having an easy time was Jim, whose evolved form allowed him to grip and hold onto branches and limbs that Ruthie and Rufus could never dream of reaching.

On and on they journeyed, into the intensifying darkness. The trees were now lined with black veins and dark patches. Thorny rattan plants had taken over, their sharp hooks waiting to snag anything in their path.

From far above them came a loud hooting, and Ruthie broke into a smile. "That's my boys; they've found the entrance!" She responded with hoots of her own, then listened intently as a series of whoops and clicks responded to her call. As she leaned back and closed her eyes, listening, Jim stared at her in awe. He hoped one day soon he would return to normal so he could take her into his arms and kiss her.

Ruthie's next words brought him out of his daydream.

"There's danger ahead," she said grimly. "We must be cautious. The gibbons have spotted what they're calling a large black... spot, whatever that means. It's moving around and seems to be waiting for us…"

✪

The path narrowed even further now, and the air became so thick that it seemed to clot into a strange, suffocating mist. Bamboo branches reached through the fog like grasping, skeletal arms.

"How much… further?" whispered Rufus, barely able to speak.

Ruthie had stopped hacking with her machete. She wiped a thin layer of black slime from the blade and slipped it into its leather sheath. "I think we've found it…"

Almost hidden by the dense chaos of bamboo trees and jungle growth was a thick chain-link fence hung with a rusted sign:

U.S. GOVERNMENT – KEEP OUT!

"Well, this certainly fits the description," said Jim, looking for some way past the fence. "Hopefully there'll be a gap or a… what did you call it? Secret entrance!"

Ruthie nodded her head, but something had disturbed her. "It's gone quiet," she said. "I can't hear the bugs. It's like everything just… stopped."

The air grew suddenly cold, and the sun disappeared, leaving the rainforest dark and still. Ruthie and Jim looked at each other as they both heard rustling in the undergrowth.

Shtoom!

A splintered bamboo spear flew out of the mist, barely missing Ruthie.

Shtoom! Shtoom! Another two spears pierced the ground at Ruthie's feet.

"Jeez–?" cried Ruthie, ducking to the side.

Several black shapes appeared out of the mist. They took aim as Jim grabbed his hockey stick from his duffle bag. He swung the metal stick at the black figures – and it passed through them, making them swirl in the eddy. He managed to hit one of the spears in the backswing, shattering it into a cloud of bamboo splinters.

Two more shadowy figures appeared, both armed with spears. Jim grabbed Rufus and Ruthie, one friend in each hand, and threw them onto his shoulders. He glanced at Wira and nodded – they understood each other perfectly.

"How are we supposed to fight shadows in this *darkness*?" cried Rufus as he hung on tightly. "We don't stand a chance if we can't actually *see* them!"

Jim followed Wira's lead and swung up into the bamboo trees, carrying Ruthie and Rufus' weight with ease. Large shafts of bamboo shot into the murk above, and Jim leaped and climbed like an acrobat, higher and higher as he dodged the whizzing spears. He was beginning to appreciate the advantages of this brutish new form; it made him even faster, more agile, more powerful.

The shadowy figures followed them, throwing spear after spear. *Shtoom! Shtoom!* Two more projectiles shot past. They flew straight at Jim, making him mistime his next swing. The branch he was hanging onto snapped under the weight, and the trio fell in a shower of leaves. Jim grabbed at another branch as Rufus and Ruthie held on to his back for dear life.

"Got ya!" he cried, almost enjoying himself, as he grabbed another branch. Jim climbed even faster and further into the trees, followed closely by Wira who effortlessly kept up. The shadow creatures fell behind, and with one last-chance hurl of a bamboo spear, they were gone.

"Aargh!" Jim yelped as a final spear struck his arm, narrowly missing Ruthie's leg. Ruthie pulled it out with a short sharp yank and watched in awe as Jim kept swinging and jumping through the trees to escape.

14. Shadows in the
NIGHT

After about an hour of swinging through the treetops, they finally landed in an opening lit by the glow of the full moon. Jim made sure the jungle floor was safe and stable before lowering Rufus and Ruthie from his back. Wira was waiting for them on a narrow ridge overlooking the jungle. There in the distance lay the granite peak of Mount Kinabalu, looming over a thick layer of cloud as the sun was starting to set.

"Wow," said Rufus quietly. "Spectacular!"

Jim nodded in agreement. "I think we lost them…"

Ruthie dug through her pack and pulled out a first aid kit for Jim's wound. The spear hadn't done much damage, it even seemed to be healing on its own but she applied an ointment to the wound anyway. Jim gave her a warm smile of thanks as she patted his cheek in return.

"I think we should just camp here for the night," she said. "Like Rufus said, there's no use trying to look for those shadows in the dead of night. We should rest and refuel and head out at first light." Ruthie handed Rufus a hammock, a sheet of tarpaulin and four bungee cords.

"Comfy!"

"Be grateful, mister – you'll thank me later!"

Walking along the two-metre wide ridge, Rufus and Ruthie found a sturdy tree trunk and strung up one end of both their hammocks.

"Right! Attach this end to that tree over there and make sure it's as level as you can get it," said Ruthie. "We don't want all your blood rushing to your brainy head, do we? It might burst! Or you rolling down a mountain now in the middle of the night?"

"Um… thanks..."

"No problem" said Ruthie, breaking into a flurry of swift and precise movements as she slung a sheet of tarpaulin over a stretched bungee cord above her hammock. She attached the delicate mosquito net like a web underneath. The whole operation was completed in seconds.

"Follow that!" she said with a smirk.

Rufus grabbed a bungee cord and mimicked Ruthie stretching the cord between the tree with the end of the hammock and the tree slightly below on the steep slope.

Ping!

"Oops!" Rufus looked sheepishly at Ruthie as one of his cords span like a flying snake into the mists way below.

"Careful – we don't have spares!" Ruthie said. "You'll

have to do the best you can with what you have left."

After battling with his hammock, bungee cords, a tarpaulin and – briefly – a curious pit viper that slithered down the back of the tree between his hands as he was tying the hammock to it, Rufus was finally finished.

"There's no way I'm getting out of this hammock once I'm in it – not with these snakes all over the place," Rufus whispered. "Who knows what else is out there… I've got a bad feeling about this…"

It wasn't long before the team had set up their camp for the night. Ruthie's wood fire burned away, sending plumes of grey smoke into the night sky.

"At least this might keep the biting bugs away," muttered Ruthie.

"You certainly know all the tricks!" said Rufus, trying to sound cheerful. "How on earth did you start that roaring fire in this wet atmosphere?"

"Secrets, Rufus! Secrets!" winked Ruthie with a smile. "And a little training." She turned her attention to a pot of bubbling stew.

Jim, on the other hand, was discovering his inner Wild Man, keeping watch on the camp from the trees above. As he wove the leaves and branches into the V of a tree, fashioning a makeshift nest, a thought struck him: he was getting used to being an orangutan…

✪

"What *were* those things?" Rufus asked. "They were like men made of shadows, like they were real but not real. Almost as though they were walking black holes…"

Ruthie took a sip of water. "They're something new. We need to explore that Shadowlab and find out what happened to my brother. I can't help feeling that the answers are there. Someone – or something – clearly doesn't want us to succeed."

"Did you feel the cold when they came near?" Rufus said. "That cold was not natural."

Ruthie shuddered and fell into a silence.

✪

It was late – their hammocks were set up precariously on a steep ridge in the misty jungle. The embers of the campfire cast an orange glow that threw strangely enlarged shadows around the clearing, reminding Jim of a Chinese shadow puppet show. He couldn't sleep. Satisfied that his friends were safe below, Jim looked up and out across the jungle canopy. The milky-blue peak of Mount Kinabalu hovered on the horizon, remote and mysterious.

Distant thunder grumbled.

Suddenly, the Headhunter Skull began to glow. It lifted out of Jim's bag and hung in the night air. "Beware, Wild Man!" it said in the familiar voice of Sengalang. "The darkness is approaching! The calm before the storm is almost at an end. Be vigilant!" With that, the skull grew dark once more. Then it fell into Jim's lap.

"What did it say?" Rufus called out from below. The skull must have woken him up.

"I think we're in for some trouble," Jim shouted in reply, "and soon. I'll keep an eye out for danger, you two go back to sleep."

"What about you?" asked Ruthie, who had also stirred from under her tarpaulin. "Don't you need to sleep?"

"I'm not tired," Jim replied. "Too much going on in here," he added, tapping his head with one large finger. "I'll take first watch and then when I start to get tired I'll wake one of you."

Ruthie nodded and lay back down in her hammock. Rufus looked at Jim questioningly before climbing back within the protection of his mosquito net and fell asleep, exhausted.

Jim settled into his nest. He suddenly felt very alone.

This has been some wild ride, he thought. *And it's not over yet. Not by a long shot...*

✪

An hour later, Jim lay on his side looking down at the camp, almost hypnotized by the monotony of the never-changing landscape. He started to drift off to sleep, so blinked a few times to keep himself awake.

From a few feet in front of him a pair of eyes blinked back.

"What–?" Jim whispered, leaning forward.

Another pair of eyes appeared. Then four more, then eight, then sixteen. Jim rubbed his eyes with his large fists. A chill crawled up his spine. What was he seeing? It was as if the blackness of night had turned a glowing shade of blue.

Shaking his head, he tried to clear his vision. He looked down, his friends were still there but Wira was nowhere to be seen.

Jim now saw blue glowing flecks out the corner of his eye. They looked like unearthly fireflies, and soon he was surrounded by them. The lights swirled and pulsated in a hypnotic dance. His eyes grew tired as he watched the spectacle, but he could not look away no matter how heavy his eyelids felt…

HAHAHAHAHAHAHAHAHAHAA!

The familiar laugh came out of nowhere, piercing the quiet and the dark. Once it faded there was only the chirrup of the insects and the light of the jungle moon.

The blue flecks were gone. And so was Jim.

15. Rufus to the RESCUE!

The camp was still as dawn broke through the leafy canopy, bathing the jungle in warm light. Insects buzzed about and animals stirred, but neither Ruthie nor Rufus moved. It was as if they had been frozen in time. One of the gibbons, Tingkar, was watching the clearing nervously, his head bobbing to and fro as he waited. There was a rustling in the trees behind him, and he spun around to see Wira looking exhausted and upset.

The orangutan sat down in the shade of a leaf beaded with morning dew. His long spindly arms flopped like jelly at his side as he greedily sucked in cool gulps of air. After resting a few seconds he began waving his arms at Tingkar.

They both swung down from the high branches to the ridge where Ruthie had set up camp the night before. Tingkar lifted the gossamer mosquito net and shook Rufus roughly.

No response.

Rufus' body was floppy and lifeless.

Wira shook Ruthie. Again, nothing.

They both looked at each other, puzzled. Tingkar slapped a gangly arm across his head as if to say, *What now?* Wira, on the other hand, looked pleased with himself. He grabbed a delicate fern and started tickling both Rufus and Ruthie in the ear and nose. But...

Still nothing.

Tingkar was now a confused tangle of arms and legs, sticking his finger in Rufus' ear and blowing on his face. All to no avail.

After a few seconds resting his chin on his fist, Wira leapt into the air, somersaulting. It seemed as though he'd had a brainwave...

The orangutan stood with his legs wide apart and his knees slightly bent. He extended his long arms, finally cracking his spindly fingers back on themselves, and climbed onto Rufus' hammock. He grabbed Rufus' head by the ears then shook vigorously.

It wasn't long before Rufus was sitting bolt upright beneath his tarpaulin, his eyes blinking in the early morning glow. "Wha... where..." he swallowed, his throat dry and sore. "What happened?" he rasped. "Where are Jim and Ruthie?"

Rufus looked over at Ruthie, who lay motionless.

He listened for her breath but couldn't hear it.

Wira shook his head at Rufus and playfully slapped Tingkar in the face. Rufus now understood what had happened. He felt his own face burning, and asked Wira, "Is that how you woke me up?" Wira nodded. "Why won't she wake?"

The orangutan spun on the spot, then darted into a tree. Using only his back legs, he hung from the tree and placed his hands over his eyes to mimic binoculars.

"Someone was watching us?" Rufus asked.

Wira nodded, and started to swing from tree to tree, going faster and faster as he circled the campsite. Rufus watched him, impressed at the little creature's ingenuity and cleverness. As Wira approached Jim's treetop nest, he clapped his arms around his body several times – then leapt up like a rocket.

Rufus finally understood what Wira was trying to say. "Jim's been taken," he said carefully, "and it sounds like it had to be the Tribe of Shadows." Wira and Tingkar nodded their heads, then hung them in sadness. Rufus climbed up to Jim's bed, digging through his duffle bag. He spotted the hockey stick and puck, rope, a torch – then realised the most important item was also gone.

"No!" Rufus cried. "They took the Headhunter Skull!"

As Rufus tried to wake Ruthie, four gibbon spies – Tiger, Ringgit, Milo, and Peng – dropped out of the trees in a tight circle, like ninjas ready to strike. Wira hooted and signed with the gibbons, bringing them up to speed on what had happened. Wira then turned to Rufus and performed his familiar charades.

"Jim… captured… taken… shadows? lab?" Rufus slowly pieced the information together. "But what about Ruthie?"

Milo and Peng started gathering up Ruthie's belongings and dismantling the makeshift camp. Before long the gibbons were loaded with bags, while Rufus swung Jim's hefty duffle bag over his shoulder. Two of the gibbons grabbed Ruthie's legs, while the other two lifted her torso.

They then took off without a further sound into the jungle, leaving Wira and Rufus alone.

Rufus scratched his head as he watched them go, then pushed his glasses higher up on his nose. "So," he said, "I guess it's safe to assume they're taking her back to *The Moody Cow*?"

When Wira nodded, Rufus pointed to himself, then at the orangutan. "It's you and me now, Wira. Think you're up for it? We have to rescue Jim and… and… well, I am not sure what comes after that."

Wira nodded emphatically. He pointed to Rufus and then himself, confirming they were now a team.

Rufus walked over to the cliff edge and stared across at the looming hulk of Mount Kinabalu, as bright and multi-faceted as a diamond in the morning sunshine. "Hmm. It's an awfully long way to walk…"

As he and Wira gazed at the mountain, the sky began to bruise. Within seconds it was dark purple and streaked with black clouds. Thunder rumbled in the distance and a mist still hung in the valleys like a white carpet. Rufus looked down at his new partner. "Do you really think the two of us stand a chance? I'm a city boy. But I guess you are the jungle expert, huh?"

Wira jumped onto Rufus' back, his warm orangutan potbelly pressed into Rufus' shoulders. He wrapped an arm around Rufus' forehead like a hairy sweatband.

"Okay, okay, we'll do it!" laughed Rufus.

As the two set off on their journey, a pair of black hornbills flew overhead, their wings displacing the hot air with a loud *Whump! Whump! Whump!* Rufus looked up, and as he did so the thunder came again.

Was it his imagination, or did the thunder sound like laughter?

✪

"Those things are alive," muttered Rufus as he and Wira tramped passed a rattan palm, its filaments reaching out to catch them with their vicious barbs. "It's like they're after our flesh…"

Suddenly a large tree root whipped up like a snake and entangled itself around Rufus' ankle. "Gah! What the heck…? Get it off me!"

As Rufus struggled to free himself he fell forward onto

his face in the dirt. Wira had hopped from Rufus' shoulders just before he hit the ground. The orangutan scrambled inside Jim's duffle bag and grabbed a can of super strength bug repellent.

Before Rufus could see what Wira was up to, the roots were engulfed in a thick cloud of acrid spray. The sinewy tendrils recoiled instantly.

As he stood brushing himself down and panting to get his breath back, Rufus became aware of a gentle churning sound off in the near distance.

"I think… there's a river ahead of us," he said to Wira between laboured breaths. "We could… follow it to Mount Kinabalu!"

Wira hooted happily and ran off into the trees to investigate. Rufus took the opportunity to rest. He was soaked in sweat. He wiped his face with a damp rag and let his heart rate return to normal.

"I am so not ready for this," he said quietly to himself. "I hope I can do this… Stop it, McFly! Jim's in trouble. Pull yourself together!"

Wira came back into the clearing and hooted excitedly. He pointed back toward the river and gave Rufus a thumbs-up. Rufus took a big swig of water and gave Wira a high five.

"Great – a boat! We can make up some serious time and go by river. That's got to be easier than walking the whole way there."

Wira whooped in agreement as Rufus repositioned the duffle bag on his shoulder, then followed Wira towards the river.

16. Over the
EDGE

The air cooled as they approached the sound of water, and soon Rufus and Wira were standing on the banks of a wide river. Warm sunlight forked its way through the canopy and alighted on a dilapidated old boat. Rufus knew the boat was their only chance of navigating the water. He certainly didn't fancy swimming...

Rufus walked over to the boat and dropped Jim's duffle bag on the jungle floor. Pushing and straining and turning bright red, he eventually pried the boat from its muddy mooring and dragged it to the water. He then inspected the boat for cracks and holes, coming to the conclusion that it was old but sound. Wira ran his hands over the rough wood, slapping the side of the boat in approval.

They soon found the oars, which were almost entirely buried in the mud-bank. Rufus slid the boat to the edge of the river and cautiously stepped in. The boat wobbled under his weight. He slowly lowered himself onto the small slatted seat at the back. After a moment, he breathed a sigh of relief.

"I had a strange feeling I was going to get wet!" he smiled. Wira, looking happy and satisfied, stretched out his long right arm and balled his hand into a fist. Rufus nervously laughed. "Right, Wira, it's just you and me versus the world!"

✪

The river's current took hold of the boat and swept it into boiling white waters. Rufus and Wira wound their way from rapid to rapid, from fast and vigorous rushes to deathly calm lulls, while Rufus struggled to keep control of the little craft. Onward they bounced, skimming large rocks that jutted from the water like monster's teeth. The white water swirled past twisted trees, fallen branches and orange blossom that hid in the mist-laden canopy above.

The river got faster and narrower, snaking its way through the jungle. The water was flowing downriver, faster and faster through a deadly flume of smooth black granite. Both Rufus and Wira remained silent as they hung on for dear life, getting soaked as they were hit by blast after blast of icy cold water. Wira looked up then clambered his way over to Rufus, helping to hold the oars out wide to slow the boat.

CRACK! The left oar dragged along the wall of stone, hit a rock at full speed – and shattered into pieces. The boat began to rotate, slowly at first, then faster and faster, the sheer rock wall coming closer and closer.

Rufus felt the full force of gravity pulling the boat down into the eye of the whirlpool. Down and round they spun, going so fast that Rufus turned several shades of green. "Hang on, Wira!" he shouted. "Oh god, I'm going to be *siiiiiick*!"

There was a loud sucking noise below them as the boat fell through the centre of the funnel, dropping them ten feet into a deep black pool of water. They were now in an immense cave of shiny, jet-black rock. Luminescent green plant life grew on the walls, and dangling lianas hung from above. The roots of the distorted trees growing above were feeding into the pool like black serpents.

As Rufus and Wira adjusted to their surroundings, drips of black water fell from the roof of the cavern, one drip after another.

"Yuck, what was that?" Rufus asked, wiping his face. He began to itch – and no matter how much he scratched, the feeling would not go away. Then, in the distance, Rufus saw a light at the end of the tunnel, bright white against the darkness. Gradually, the current drew them on towards the source of the illumination.

"Uh oh," said Rufus as he brushed something from his face and saw that it was a swarm of tiny black spiders. Within seconds, thousands of the arachnids began to fall on Rufus and Wira, covering them and everything in the small boat.

The light grew brighter, the opening grew larger, the spiders kept falling and the rush of water got louder. Rufus was stood precariously in the boat as he flailed around trying to knock off as many of the arachnids as he could. Amid the chaos, Rufus swore that he could hear sinister laughter echoing around the cave. In the corner of his eye he saw hideous shadow-creatures twisting their way along the jagged cave-walls. But then he realised – it was his own shadow, dancing grotesquely as he flailed about in the boat.

"*I hate spideeeeeeeeeeeeeeeeeeeerrrrrrrrrrrrrrssss!*"

Rufus' screams were ripped from his lungs as the little wooden boat finally hit the wall of light and tipped. Rufus looked dead ahead, holding on with all his strength, his knuckles whitening, as the boat shot over the edge of the falls. Wira span round at the very last minute, leaping into the void like a spider-coated ninja.

Rufus' world went into slow motion as he watched Wira fall away into the mists. A second later Rufus himself had plunged through the fog – and the view that awaited him took his breath away. Stretched beneath Rufus, gleaming darkly in the half-light, was the elusive Shadowlab and its giant lightning conductor that was nestled into the cliff edge.

Rufus fell as torrents of icy cold water smothered him from above. The spiders were gone now – washed away in the deluge. Flailing and screaming – Rufus fell for what felt like an eternity, the wind sucked from his lungs. His chest was burning, gasping for air, trapped inside a wall of falling water and fear.

SPLOOSH! Rufus' fall came to an abrupt end as he splashed through the surface of a vast, icy pool. Shooting pains splintered through his body as he struggled to reach the surface past millions of air bubbles all trying to do the same.

SPLURGH! Rufus bobbed to the surface, his mouth wide open, gasping. His chest heaved as he looked about him. The waterfall was spewing foam a hundred metres above his head, sending it crashing down into the churning pool.

Rufus dragged his body to the misty bank and rolled onto his back.

"Ooohhh ee oooohhh ee ooooooo!"

Out of nowhere, Wira landed on his chest.

"You made it!" cried Rufus deliriously. "You're alive!"

"Ooh?" hooted Wira, taking the whole experience in his stride.

Leaning up on one elbow, Rufus looked around to see the shattered remains of his little boat swirling in the water, followed by Jim's duffle bag, which bobbed along encased in its waterproof liner, still tied to the metal oarlock he had tied it to earlier. Wira grabbed a broken branch reaching for the bag as Rufus waded back into the water and finally lifted it onto dry land.

///

Rufus dug around in the duffle bag for the torn fragment of map Ruthie had given back to Jim. He held it up to the light for Wira and himself to examine. They found where the waterfalls were located in the foothills of Mount Kinabalu, and before their eyes, strange markings began to form on the map. The symbols glowed, spreading like luminous tree roots across the chart. They led from the waterfalls into the mountain and converged on the "X" that Ruthie had drawn on the map.

"That must be the exact location of the Shadowlab's entrance!" Rufus said, scratching his chin. "Right? I mean, what else could it be?" Wira reached up and plucked the map from Rufus' fingers, studying it for himself.

"According to this there's an entrance around here somewhere," Rufus said, pushing his glasses higher up on his nose, his eyes scanning the featureless grey rock.

"But… where?"

Both he and Wira began walking around the riverbank searching the base of the cliff for some sort of hidden doorway. After a few long minutes they could not spot anything visible, and there did not seem to be a way to get around the waterfall unless they swam.

Rufus noticed how cold it was this close to the waterfall, and how no insects or birds came near it. As he studied the water intently, Wira tugged on his shorts and pointed to the darkness behind the waterfall. Both of them moved closer to the mountain's surface and saw the entrance hidden by the rushing water. A chill ran down Rufus' spine. This place felt evil. "Well, I think we found our secret entrance, Wira." The orangutan hooted in agreement. Rufus picked up Jim's duffle bag and slung it over his shoulders. Then, skirting past the crashing water of the falls, they stepped into darkness together.

17. The

DARK MATTER SCOPE

The world was pitch black. Jim couldn't see, but he knew something was very wrong. All he could remember was a bright blue glow, then this all-enveloping darkness. His wrists and ankles hurt, and he wondered if they were sore from being restrained. Strange electronic noises echoed around him, and he could make out a bubbling sound as well. His nose was filled with an acrid smell. He couldn't move his body. He had a nasty feeling that he was trapped.

From out of the void, Jim heard the sound of strong but halting footsteps on a metallic floor. They stopped – and then Jim felt a fiery pain flowing up his left arm.

"Aaaargh! Who's there? Who's *doing* this to me?" he screamed.

The pain was intense, and it felt as if something was being leeched out of him.

"Easy, Wild Man!" The stranger's voice was cold and raspy. "You don't want this to hurt more than it already does."

Jim felt another sharp pain as he was injected with something. Light penetrated the darkness. Finally, his eyes began to adjust to his surroundings. His body came alive as well, and he moved his arms and legs, testing their strength. But still he couldn't break the straps that held him down. He blinked repeatedly. White light flooded into his eyes and he began to make out patterns and shapes moving around him.

"This will hurt, I promise you," said the voice.

The pain was excruciating. Jim screamed. As his vision cleared, he realised that he was strapped to a cold metal operating table, which seemed to be floating on a thick layer of white mist.

A shadowy figure loomed just outside his field of vision.

A large probe was attached to his left arm, extracting his blood.

"Welcome back... *Protector*!" spat the voice.

"Who are you?" Jim whispered.

"I am asking the questions. You are the last of the Protectors, are you not?"

Jim sighed. "What?"

"Do not try to trick me, Wild Man."

"I don't know what you're talking about," said Jim.

"LIAR!"

The black figure moved into view and for the first time Jim saw that its face was hidden beneath a hood.

"I speak of that tribe of Headhunters and their insolent, manipulative medicine man…"

"Headhunters? Medicine man? What do you want with *me*?" Jim demanded. Now he could see a machine in the centre of the room. It was covered in lights and surrounded by vials of bubbling liquid.

"Are you looking for this?" the shadowy figure asked, pointing to another machine. This one held the Headhunter Skull in an illuminated glass chamber. The skull, like Jim, was shrouded in white mist. "Don't think that Sengalang and his hoodoo skull will be able to save you. I have blocked its neural pathways, and no amount of telepathy or mind control will be able to penetrate this chamber."

The figure laughed.

"Time is running out for you and your precious friends. As soon as the Dark Matter absorbs the power of the Orang-ee from you, we shall rise from the depths and destroy this fragile planet you call home and build a new empire, a Kingdom of Shadows! Nothing can stop the Shadow Emperor now. Doctor Gila, Master of Darkness, will reign supreme!"

"You're insane," said Jim. "Master of Darkness? Where did you come up with that? You don't stand a ch–Aaaarrgghh!"

A shock of electricity shot through Jim's body, making him convulse and shudder. Every strand of his hair stood on end. The pain stopped for a few seconds, then jolted through him again.

"Aaaarrgghh!"

"I will break you, Wild Man! You will give me your secrets before you die… But right now, I want you to meet someone. Someone with incredible powers of persuasion. The Huntress!"

Out of the darkness came a beautiful dark-haired Malaysian woman clad in black. Yellow piping highlighted her armour, and she moved with a quiet, deadly grace.

"I am here, Doctor Gila." She moved toward Jim and smiled at him, her eyes glowing yellow. "Don't you recognise me?"

Jim searched his memory but could not place her. "No," he said, confused.

"The black dog. The old man smoking his pipe. I know where you have been, and who your feisty young friend is…"

"Ruthie! Don't you harm her!"

"Don't worry, Wild Man, she is safe… for now. And for how long? That is up to you."

The Huntress had a gleeful look in her eyes." I look forward to breaking her, too. Cracking her resolve, destroying her beautiful mind. But not until I destroy yours first!"

Doctor Gila held up a gloved hand. "Do what you must,

Huntress, but I want him alive… mostly." Doctor Gila laughed coldly as he left the room. "Break his spirit and mind, but I want his body intact."

"As you wish, my master."

The Huntress stood and stared at Jim silently, her yellow eyes hypnotising him. He tried to look away but he could not. His eyes widened in fear as her face began to change, and she became a familiar figure.

Ruthie now stood in the Huntress' place, an evil smirk on her face.

"No!"

Ruthie moved toward him seductively.

She kissed Jim tenderly.

After a few seconds the kiss began to sting, as if poison was flowing into his body and blurred his vision. When he could see clearly again she had morphed into Rufus, but this Rufus looked mean and powerful, his eyes glowing an evil shade of yellow.

"Look at you," said Rufus, laughing. "I don't need you! Why drag me into this, you red-haired freak? You're a monster, an abomination! You're no friend of mine…"

Jim stared silently at the imposter Rufus, trying to remain calm. He knew the Huntress was messing with his mind – and it was working. Every word she said had cut him like a knife. Tears welled in his eyes as he fought to control himself.

The Huntress morphed once more, but before Jim could see what shape she had taken, she disappeared into the mist that hung about the room. Jim tried to find her, but he could not see very far.

After a few moments of stillness and silence, he felt something tickle his leg and heard a skittering noise from below. Several thin black legs appeared – and then a massive black spider crawled onto the table and moved slowly toward Jim. He tried to shake it off, but it would not budge. Each of its eight legs felt like needles in his skin. It stalked its way up his giant frame, across his thick chest toward his head. One by one, each of its thin legs clamped onto his skull, holding him in position. Its mandibles clicked and dripped with venom as it sank its fangs into his neck.

"*Aaaarrgghh!*"

Pain spread like wildfire through his veins, and he heard the Huntress' voice in his head.

"*Revalationsssss,*" she hissed. "Open your mind to me, Wild Man!"

Jim clenched his eyes shut to block out the spider, and his mouth opened in a defiant roar. "*Never!*"

✪

Hours later, the spider jumped down from the table and into the mists. Jim lay on the table, panting and exhausted, feeling utterly drained. Two black shadows loomed above him: sentries guarding his body, menacing and silent.

Jim turned his head wearily and looked at all the machinery around him. Tubes from his body fed his blood into the machine's countless empty vials. He saw his bio readouts on another monitor screen as they analysed his DNA, and a heart monitor kept tabs of his heartbeat.

The Huntress emerged from the shadows once again, back in her human form. She connected herself to one of the machines, and glanced over her shoulder at Jim.

She pushed a button. Electrical current shot through Jim's broken body and mind.

Jim screamed, trying to stay awake. "Why?" he croaked in a small voice.

The Huntress' wordless response sent another surge of electrical pain through his body.

Jim's world went black once more.

18. The Guardian of the
BRIDGE

Rufus and Wira stepped into the cave. Their senses were assaulted from every direction. It was cold, echoing with strange noises – and the strong smell of guano filled their noses. After a few steps, the little amount of light thrown out by the waterfall began to fade, and they were soon swallowed by darkness.

Rufus dug into the duffle bag for Jim's torch. "I hope there are no more mutated creatures staring at us right now. I think I've had enough of monster bugs!" He found the torch and clicked it on.

"This place is massive," he noted, looking around in awe. He tried to find Wira in the torch's beam, but the little orangutan was nowhere to be seen. "Wira!" he cried, "Where are you?"

Wira popped up and made the orangutan equivalent of "Boo!"

"Oh God!" Rufus cried – then calmed down once he sensed Wira had tricked him. The orangutan was practically rolling on the ground in laughter. "You scared me!" Rufus said, trying not to laugh himself. "Not funny! Bad monkey!"

Wira jumped back on to Rufus' shoulders, and the two made their way further into the cave. Rufus tried to illuminate their path, but there was a thick haze in the air. The cave was immense, a cathedral of spire-like rock formations. As Rufus shone the torch around the structure, he spotted several tunnel openings lit by strange glowing lichen.

"Look over there, Wira," he said. "Which one should we take?"

There was a fluttering sound from above, and as Rufus shone the torch toward the ceiling of the cave, his heart dropped. Thousands of red eyes stared back at him. Something large and leathery flew past Rufus, startling Wira, who began flailing his arms.

"Bats!"

The cave quickly became a fluttering, flapping maelstrom of leathery bat wings and screeches. The creatures flew in and out of the light as Rufus covered his face with his arms, trying to protect himself. Wira had hopped off his back and was doing the same. Rufus reached for his friend and accidentally dropped the torch. It clattered to the ground and clicked off, plunging their world once more into blackness.

"No!" cried Rufus, as he got down on all fours and groped in the darkness for the torch. He found it, clicked it on. As a strong beam of light lit up the cave, Rufus smiled. But then he noticed how wet and sticky the torch was…

"Bat poo!" he cried. "Gross!" He tried wiping his hands on the cave wall, then gave up and used the leg of his shorts instead. "Ugh! Disgusting!"

As he started to wipe the torch clean, he noticed something and called Wira over. "Look at the wall," he told the orangutan. "When I move the beam of light away from the openings in the cave there's a strange glowing arrow left on the wall. How crazy is that? I guess we discovered the way to go…"

Rufus and Wira moved slowly along the twisting path toward the left opening that was still illuminated by the glowing arrow. As they moved into the opening a warm wind blew through the tunnels, followed soon after by a waft of cold air.

"Did you notice how the air smelled?" he asked Wira. "Metallic. Maybe it's some kind of extraction vent?"

The path wound on through the mountain, the walls becoming wetter, blacker and more treacherous as they travelled. The walls skittered and teemed with cockroaches and dozens of other centipedes and bugs, all searching for food or places to burrow.

For several hours they kept walking, pausing only to sip

water from their bottles and eat some protein bars and nuts. The tunnels got narrower and narrower the further they travelled, but every divide in their path was lit with a glowing arrow that pointed them in the right direction. The path wound its way upward past rocky outcroppings and finally ended in a large chasm that prevented them from going any further.

Right in front of them was a vast canyon lit from above by small openings in the ceiling. Shafts of blue glowing light filled the cave, illuminating the stalactites that hung from above like immense spikes. A rickety slatted bridge spanned the chasm, and as Rufus and Wira looked over the cliff edge to the blackness below, they could see nothing but mist and darkness. Rufus kicked a stone into the void, but they didn't hear it hit the bottom, no matter how hard they listened…

The two stared at each other, then at the rickety bridge. They knew what they had to do.

Rufus stepped tentatively onto the bridge. The ropes looked frayed, and several of the planks were missing. Wira jumped on Rufus' back as he made his way further onto the bridge. There was an uneasy creak of wood as the bridge took Rufus and Wira's full weight.

"Please hold, please hold, please hold, please hold," Rufus whisper-chanted as they slowly made their way further and further across the bridge. "Don't look down, Wira!"

One step turned into two, five turned into ten, and before long they were almost halfway across the bridge. By then Rufus' knees had turned to jelly and he was shaking badly. He took a deep breath and tried to calm himself as sweat ran down his face and back. More and more planks were missing the further they went, forcing Rufus to make larger steps across the chasm. He accidentally glanced down and found himself staring at the swirling mists below.

"Oh God," whimpered Rufus. "I looked down." Wira slapped his hand against his forehead.

A rumble like thunder came from the cave tunnel behind them, and as they continued on their way another rumble sounded. Rufus paused on the creaking plank which he was now stood on, which was straining under the combined weight of himself and Wira, and tried to look back in the direction they had come from.

"Wh– what was that noise?"

The rumble was getting louder and closer, and before they could take another step, a large black mass of jelly armed with a gaping mouth of serrated teeth appeared at the tunnel opening and tested the air with its antennae.

"What... the... hell... *is*... that?" whispered Rufus. "Is that a... *leech*?"

As soon as Rufus spoke he realised the mistake he had made, as the creature reared its head in their direction seeking out the source of the noise. It jolted and turned its bulk toward them, its teeth grinding in its massive mouth, then slammed its tail onto the ground. The shockwave shook the bridge and hit Rufus and Wira like a truck.

The mutated leech pulsed and rippled toward them with surprising speed, working its way onto the bridge. Its massive body barely fit between the ropes as it worked its way toward Rufus and Wira.

Creak! Crack!

The bridge bowed under the weight of the giant creature, and Rufus realised that he and Wira would never make it across in time, so fumbled with a stray bit of rope around his wrist. He tried to get his legs to move faster, but they seemed to have turned to jelly and were not responding.

The creature loomed near them, rearing up on its bulk into one of the shafts of blue light coming from above. Its body was covered in tiny ripples slick with black slime, its teeth shone bright, dripping with drool.

Rufus looked up at the rows and rows of teeth looming above him and knew that this was it. As a splash of the creature's drool hit his cheek, he closed his eyes and prepared for the end. Wira wrapped himself tight around Rufus' neck and buried his face in Rufus' hair.

As the creature lowered itself to swallow Rufus and Wira whole, the bridge ropes finally snapped with a *toing!*

Rufus and Wira fell as the bridge snapped in half. Rufus' arms were still wrapped around the rope, and he hung on for dear life as his half of the bridge swung toward the far wall of the cave.

The mutant leech plummeted into the mists below as Rufus and Wira slammed into the rock face with a loud crash. Several of the loose wooden slats fell away and tumbled past them as they held on with all their might.

The bridge stopped swaying and creaking, and Rufus and Wira shakily made their way up the remains of the bridge, climbing it like a ladder, then heaved themselves onto the cave floor at the top. They sat panting for a full five minutes.

"That," Rufus said eventually, "was *disgusting!*"

19. The Gathering
STORM

Ruthie finally awoke, her eyes adjusting to light again and her head felt heavy and woozy. "What happened?" she asked groggily. "Oh, my head hurts…"

She rubbed her temples with the palm of her hands and her vision returned to normal. She looked around and struggled to place her surroundings. She was in a darkened room with wood panelled walls and almost no furniture. A lime-coloured gecko scurried across the ceiling. "Where am I?"

"It is okay, Moody Cow Lady," came a creaky old voice from the dark.

Ruthie turned her head toward the disembodied voice, and saw the small man seated cross-legged on a rattan mat in a shady corner of the candle-lit room. His eyes were closed, and he looked like he was meditating.

"I am Sengalang. Iban shaman, lah…"

"I know who you are, but how did I–?"

"Let me speak!" Sengalang opened his eyes, and Ruthie

noticed that they looked sad. "Your friend, our Protector, has been taken, lah? Our werangutan, the Iban Protector, has been kidnapped by a malevolent force that lurks beneath our mountain. Mount Kinabalu is hiding a secret that finally wants to rear its evil head. All we know is that the Tribe of Shadows, a dangerous group of mutated creatures, moulded by evil itself, has been created to destroy all of what we love and cherish. Our world is growing dark, twisted by the Shadows. I fear that we are not ready to face it. Our Saviour is gone, and a mighty storm is brewing. Our hopes are fading fast... we *must* find the Protector!"

"So you are the one responsible for turning Jim into this... werangutan, is it?" Ruthie asked, getting angry.

"He has been turned by ancient Iban magic into our most noble Earth Protector. I have been watching him from afar, guiding him to this point in time, lah..."

Ruthie clenched her fists and tensed. "You've been manipulating him, you mean! Did you stop to think about his life, his career, his path, before you made that decision?!"

Sengalang held up a hand to silence her. "We need him. You need him. The *world* needs him!" He paused for a moment to let his words sink in. He untangled his crossed legs and rose. He walked over to where Ruthie was sitting and took her hands in his. "You have a part to play here. You must rescue Jim. We cannot do it, for we have been cursed and our crops are dying, our food is spoiling and the river is drying up. We cannot go past a certain point in the jungle. *You* must help him."

"What about the skull that Jim has? Is that part of the plan, too?"

"The Headhunter Skull of Orang-eee! Let us hope he still has it, as all will be lost if it falls into the wrong hands. It will aid the Protector on his journey, but it could also become a weapon in the claws of evil…"

Their conversation was interrupted by the sudden arrival of Noodle, whose fur was singed and matted with blood. He stumbled over to Ruthie and collapsed into her arms.

"Noodle! What happened? Where's Maggi?" she asked in a panic. "Who did this to you?" The gibbon hooted and signed Ruthie his story. Tears welled in her eyes, she hugged the animal close and turned away. "Oh no, no no no… Oh, Maggi…"

"What has happened?" asked Sengalang.

"*The Moody Cow* has been breached," said Ruthie. "Noodle says a vicious black dog-like creature went on a rampage. The flood defences were broken and some of my lower rooms are all flooded and useless. One minute the creature attacked Maggi and Noodle, then the next a woman appeared, plugged herself into the central computer, and fried the system." Ruthie sighed deeply. "Maggi was killed. They didn't stand a chance. I should have been there!"

Sengalang placed a comforting hand on Ruthie's shoulder as she cried. She held Noodle close, and shook with sorrow as Tingkar, Tiger, Ringgit, Milo and Peng came into the room and gathered around her.

"I am truly sorry for your losses. It must have something to do with the Tribe of Shadows and the evil of the Shadowlab. We must remain strong, defiant... ready to counter the darkness with light!"

Sengalang moved to the barred window and looked out at Mount Kinabalu. Dark menacing clouds were gathering at its peak. "A storm is coming, and we must stop it."

He walked back to his mat in the corner of the room and sat, his eyes closed in thought and pain.

Ruthie buried her face in Noodle's fur as the other gibbons tried to comfort her. "Oh, Albert," she whispered through her tears. "Albert, what have you done?"

20. Beneath the
SHADOWLAB

Rufus and Wira were slowly but surely making their way along the darkened cave tunnels, checking for everything and anything that could hurt them. They noticed that the slippery rocks and lichen-covered walls were getting blacker the further they went, and a root system seemed to be embedded into the rock face.

"Look at these roots, Wira," Rufus said as he shone his torch on the black tendrils that seemed to pulse from within. "That's just… creepy!"

Pods of bubbling black goo grew like pustules from the roots. "It's like this place is alive with evil."

As they moved ahead, the tunnel turned into a metal-lined corridor, lit by small down-lighters. The air was still cold, but drier, and the smell of metal replaced the more organic cave smells. In front of them was a steel door riveted with large bolts and a wheel in its centre. Rufus turned the wheel with surprising ease, and the door opened with a hiss. The air beyond was at least ten degrees cooler, making Rufus and Wira shiver.

"What is this place?" Rufus whispered.

As they stepped over the threshold a runway of lighting flickered into life, illuminating the long empty corridor ahead. The only item in the corridor was a digital screen covered in a layer of frost. Rufus wiped his hand over the screen to clear it, and a green LED light was revealed, along with the words '300: No Entry - Authorised Personnel Only'.

"I guess this must be the level number," he told Wira, who hooted in agreement. There was a faint circular pattern etched with a thin V-shaped groove made up of concentric rings and tiny circles on the floor, which intrigued Rufus as he rubbed his arms to keep warm. He looked around the room for some sort of door or elevator system, but he couldn't see anything obvious. Scratching the stubble on his chin, he thought for a moment, then decided to try a few vocal commands to see if they worked.

"Computer?" he asked hopefully. No response.

"Mother?" Rufus smirked... Nothing.

"Take me to your leader!" he said, waiting for a response. "I've always wanted to say that."

When nothing happened, Rufus tried one last command. "Beam me up?"

As soon as he finished speaking, there was a loud click as the screen came out of standby mode. A large up and down arrow appeared on the screen with a rectangle in-between, with the number 300 now in its centre. A list of all the levels appeared in order in a faint white text. Rufus' mouth hung open, blown away by the advanced technology.

"Whoa," he said. "Is this really US technology? It's really advanced but something doesn't feel… right." He looked down at Wira. "Houston? I think we have a problem."

Wira scratched his head, not understanding the reference. Rufus ran his finger down the list of named levels. Some were blank, but the others read:

Level 01 – Lightning Conductor/Communications Mast
Level 03 – Biolab
Level 101 – Toxic Waste Disposal and Storage Area
Level 298 – Dark Matter Laboratory
Level 665 – The Dark Matter Collider
Level 666 – The Dark Matter Reactor

The floor started to vibrate gently as the etching slowly filled with bright green light. Rufus' instincts told him to push a button, so he hit the down arrow and hoped for the best. *Level 665 – The Dark Matter Collider* lit up. Seconds later the floor began to glow, and a beam of lime green light engulfed Rufus and Wira, turning them both into pixelated data particles. Then they disappeared with a loud *POP!*

✪

A nanosecond later they reappeared, their bodies intact.

"Tch! It could have at least washed and dried a new set of clothes for me! What sort of hotel is this?" Rufus giggled with nervous laughter.

Below them was another of the 'crop circle' patterns. They were standing in some kind of tele-portal attached to the side of a cubicle filled with monitors and computer terminals flickering with data. The small control room seemed to float on the side of a massive curved tunnel lined with millions of delicate, thin glass tubes. Inside the tubes was more of the pulsing black goo they had encountered in the tunnel.

The only thing standing between them and the elaborate system was a clear glass door with a biohazard radioactive symbol prominent in the middle.

"Think this symbol here sums up why we are in here and not out there!" exclaimed Rufus. Wira had his face and hands pressed up against the glass like a small child looking on in wonder.

There was the sound of crackling energy from along the tunnel; a bright, silvery light was heading their way at immense speed. A sign above the door lit up: *Warning! Shielding Active.*

Rufus and Wira looked at each other – their hair stood on end as the static levels in the room increased. Rufus tried to pat his hair down, but it stood taller than any hair product he had used before.

"These electrical readings are massive – look!" Rufus watched the needle on a guage as it moved from green into orange and then into red. "My whole body is tingling!" Wira lightly touched Rufus on the leg with one long finger and a static bolt zapped them both. "Ouch! Wira, cut that out!"

A ball of silvery black light the size of a house shot past. Rufus stared at the monitors, rubbing his leg, and saw the ball's trajectory overlaid on a map of the world. It completely encircled the Pacific Ocean!

"It looks like this facility is conducting Dark Matter experiments under the most unstable and fragile part of the earth's crust… the Pacific Ring of Fire! This could be catastrophic for the planet. The area is prone to earthquakes and volcanoes normally, but whatever they are doing in this Shadowlab is going to create volcanoes and earthquakes of epic, world-killing proportions. Why would they do something like this?"

Suddenly his vision blurred and a sharp pain pulsed behind his eyes. "Gah!" he shouted, rubbing his eyes with his hands. A deep, raspy cackle echoed through Rufus' head, and a pair of evil snake-like eyes appeared in his mind.

He slammed his palms down on a view-screen to steady himself. Wira wrapped his hand around Rufus' leg to help as he shot his human friend a worried look. Rufus saw Jim lying bound to a laboratory table, surrounded by electrodes and bubbling vials of black goo.

"Jim! Jim! What is– ack!" Rufus slumped over as the mind attack ceased. "What," he said after a few ragged breaths, "was that?" He shook his head and looked at Wira. "Something bad is going on here, and Jim needs our help. He's in some sort of science lab. I think…"

Rufus walked over to the tele-portal and glowing floor circle and slammed his hand against the view-screen. "Where is he?" he yelled. "Show me!"

The screen remained blank aside from the flashing arrow next to *Level 665*. Rufus pushed the up arrow in frustration.

Level 03 – Biolab. Once again the green light engulfed them both. They reappeared in another cubicle, this time labelled with a sun symbol and a warning sign that read *Danger – Photosynthesis in Progress.*

"What could this be, Wira?" Rufus sprung over to the monitors and looked at a view of a jungle that was almost totally bleached out.

"I can't see... It said Biolab – that sounds science lab-like? Maybe a greenhouse of some kind?"

Rufus grabbed a pair of black goggles from a hook for himself – and also a pair for Wira – and put them on.

"I can't see anything now…?"

A robotic voice boomed from a speaker above their heads...

Airlock cycle in progress. Exposure commencing in 20 seconds - apply protective goggles now.

After a few seconds of blindness, Rufus and Wira's vision returned as heat and humidity engulfed them.

Brilliant white light smothered everything. It was as if they were staring into a sun – a giant ball of white light. Rufus could just make out shapes and patterns in the distance. Giant trees and leaves surrounded a vast glass dome with a large black pool in its centre. It could have been a huge underground lake for all Rufus could make out – then he saw the black sinuous roots, larger than he had seen before, sprawling across the ground and glass walls like a network of veins. The more he stared into the light, the more it made him feel nauseous. There were shadowy shapes of what looked like immense creatures, and Rufus recalled with a shiver the giant praying mantis and the mutated rafflesia plant…

There was a buzzing noise in the distance. Wira grabbed onto Rufus' leg for comfort as an army of silhouettes lumbered out of the light, heading straight for them.

Wira jumped onto Rufus' back as he stepped back into the airlock, fumbling for the button with his hand.

"Why is it not working?" Rufus couldn't take his eyes off the shapes that were coming for him.

The buzzing was getting louder and louder...

"Ooooohhh! Aaa! Aaaa! Aa!" Wira jumped off Rufus, hooting hysterically. He leapt up and slammed his palm onto the control pad.

A glass shield slid in front of them, just as a giant mutated blood-red dragonfly smashed into the glass with an almighty crash!

The stunned bug fell to the floor just as Rufus came to his senses. He noticed with mounting panic the hairline fractures that were now crawling across the glass, like evil fingers grasping for him.

Klaxons started to blare – a red light on the ceiling span wildly as a calm feminine voice blasted from a speaker.

Warning! Shield Damage – Airlock Cycle incomplete – follow emergency protocols – shield failure imminent.

"Oh sweet jeez… What is she on?" Before Rufus could say any more a huge black frog leapt onto the cracked glass – its skin secreted some form of acid on to the already damaged surface.

"Quick Wira!" Rufus was now hysterical as Wira finally got the view-screen to show the arrows.

Warning! Containment Breach! Warning!

"I know!" Rufus stared at the monstrous panorama unravelling before him.

At the last minute Rufus dragged Wira over to the floor pad as green started to flood the pattern.

There was a loud explosion as the glass shielding shattered into a million pieces, showering Rufus and Wira. There was a loud whooshing sound as the air was sucked from the room.

Wira pushed the downward arrow at the last second – and he and Rufus dissolved into green.

The last thing Rufus saw was a myriad of gaping jaws and razor sharp claws as monsters stormed the control room.

✪

Rufus and Wira rematerialised on Level 298. The Dark Matter Laboratory. But unlike the other levels, this portal was dirty, damaged, and covered in soot. The monitor was cracked, and all the other computers were either offline or broken.

"Um… this is weird," whispered Rufus. "What were they doing playing God in that *Biolab* greenhouse? What were they thinking of doing with those monsters? Pets, maybe? It's not like…" Rufus stopped in mid-sentence as he heard someone shouting on the other side of the damaged metal wall.

"GILAHHHH" a voice boomed.

Rufus looked at Wira, his eyes widening in terror.

They were not alone.

21. Werangutan
RESCUE!

"Gila!" cried the voice again.
Rufus and Wira crouched down and kept silent, eavesdropping on this sinister conversation.

"Yes, my Lord," came another voice. "We... have a problem."

"What do you mean? The ape Protector'sssss mind issss broken, yesss? He will not be able to cause ussss any more trouble."

"I'm not so sure, my Lord. There has been a disturbance on *Level 03* – the containment field has collapsed and the creatures have broken through!"

"I know thissss, you fool! I told you I can manipulate the minds of the weak. I have seen these puny infidelsss. Set the Huntresss upon them!"

"She has gone to destroy the Headhunters in their village. Our army of mutated shadow creatures is ready and at your disposal, my Lord. They are all set to spread across this island and the world beyond. All that is needed is the final command from you..."

"Excellent! First I will crusssshh the life from those meddling Headhunterss and their interfering shaman, Sengalang. Unleash the beasts and have them destroy anything in their path!"

Rufus and Wira looked at each other in horror.

"Convert the Pink Pearl into the Dark Matter Bomb," the sinister voice continued. "The time has come to unleash its power upon this pitiful world. We must combine the heart of that foolish Iban culture, this mystical white light burning at the Pearl's core, with the Dark Matter you have discovered. This will trigger the fusion needed to detonate the bomb. The time is now… The great storm is upon us! Its power will complete my transit into your universe! I have waited long enough in exile, drifting through the null space between physical realities. Nothing will prevent me from creating my Kingdom of Shadowsss… My Dark Matter Realm!"

Rufus and Wira watched as Doctor Gila stepped over to a control terminal embedded into the massive array of the Dark Matter Scope. He pressed several buttons, releasing the Pink Pearl from its prison. A robotic arm manipulated the sphere into a vertical tube of plexi-glass that closed with a hiss. The myriad of large black vials that surrounded the pearl's containment rotated slowly, releasing their bubbling Dark Matter into the chamber.

"The Dark Matter bomb is ready and primed, my Shadow Emperor," said Doctor Gila.

"The time isssss upon ussss, Gila!"

Rufus and Wira could see something looming in the portal, half-hidden. It was the front claws and scaled face of a giant lizard-like creature. *This must be the Shadow Emperor*, thought Rufus.

He noticed several Shadow Warriors looming behind the Shadow Emperor's portal, and swallowed hard. He tried to stand up to get a better look at what was going on, but his legs had fallen asleep and pins and needles shot through them. He struggled not to cry out in pain, then tripped and fell forward with a loud crash.

Wira's eyes shot open wide staring at the evil shape that appeared behind Rufus.

Rufus turned, face-to-face with a sinister cowled figure that swiped at him with its powerful arm. Rufus flew across the room, clattering into the main chamber. Doctor Gila spun around menacingly, brandishing a long black staff, his cape swirling.

"Intruderssss!" screamed the Shadow Emperor. "Deal with them!"

A silvery ball of Dark Matter shot out from the end of Doctor Gila's black staff, barely missing Rufus. Glancing down, Rufus saw a scorch mark on the side of Jim's duffle bag. He grimaced, then pulled out Jim's metal hockey stick and brandished it before him.

Wira somersaulted between Doctor Gila and Rufus

leaping onto the Dark Matter Scope, causing a distraction so that Rufus could escape. Rufus' left leg wobbled as he tried to get the rest of the cramp to go away, and as he limped toward the door, several Shadow Warriors swirled around him, trying to block his path. Suddenly filled with adrenalin, Rufus leapt into the air, in a kind of slow motion, and took a swipe at two more blasts with Jim's hockey stick. "Home Run!" shouted Rufus in shock as both Dark Matter balls strangely rebounded off the stick and ricocheted across the chamber like a pinball machine. "Woah! No Way…" he exclaimed in surprise as he landed and another ball crackled past his ear.

"Get them!" The Shadow Emperor screamed. Doctor Gila aimed his staff at Wira and fired several Dark Matter balls that missed their target and hit the machinery instead, sizzling on impact.

Gila let out a frustrated growl, then turned and limped toward Rufus, who was moving down a dark, misty corridor. Wira bounced after them, somersaulting and swinging from the roots growing through the ceiling. He soon out-manoeuvred Gila and raced down the corridor after Rufus.

The further they ran the more lost they became. Rufus looked back over his shoulder to see where their pursuers were – and then smashed into an invisible force field, which sent him flying backward onto the cold metal floor.

"Ooof! What was *that*?! This place is a death trap!"

Walls of thick opaque glass surrounded them. Rufus got back on his feet and picked up Jim's hockey stick, which had clattered to the floor. Wira was looking through the glass, trying to make out what was on the other side. He began hooting and jumping up and down, tugging on Rufus' arm.

Rufus moved along the glass wall until he came across a clear panel, then reeled in shock when he saw Jim strapped to a medical table.

He couldn't tell if his friend was unconscious or not, but Rufus hoped for the best. Finding the door control, he slapped his hand on the button and the door hissed open.

The room was quiet, and seemed to be empty apart from Jim. Rufus and Wira stepped cautiously into the space. When they were sure the coast was clear, they ran over to Jim.

Electrodes were attached to Jim's skin, and the slight smell of singed fur filled Rufus' nose as he tried nudging his friend awake.

"Jim! Jim!" Rufus shouted, "It's me! Come on, wake up!" He started to cry, his tears splashing on Jim's furry body.

Wira spotted something half-hidden by the twisted black tree roots in the corner of the room, and walked over to investigate. When he saw it was the Headhunter Skull, hanging suspended in a glass case surrounded by a white mist, he grabbed Jim's hockey stick and swung with all his might. The glass shattered and the skull rolled to the ground, where it lay staring with empty eyes.

Wira grabbed the skull and leapt onto Jim's chest, placing it in front of his face.

An orange glow began to emanate from the skull and soon surrounded the trio. Rufus and Wira covered their eyes. A voice whispered in their ears and echoed across the chamber.

"Wild Man!"

Jim's eyes suddenly popped open, and he let out a deafening roar. The leather straps stretched and snapped as Jim stood on the table and let out a battle cry while hammering his fists on his chest. Blue light filled his eyes as Jim held the skull aloft.

Seconds later Jim noticed his best friend and Wira cowering a few feet away. He broke into another roar – this time of happy laughter. He leaped from the table and grabbed Rufus and Wira into a huge monster hug.

22. The Huntress
ATTACKS

Sengalang stared into the fire that crackled away before him as he recited ancient texts under his breath. His skin glowed in the firelight, and he barely moved. Through the smoke he could see the decapitated wooden orangutan statue that was destroyed when Jim arrived in Borneo.

A circle of Headhunters sat in prayer around the edge of the sacred clearing. All Ruthie could hear was a strange muttering, a chanting of sorts, from the circle of one hundred praying men.

The Iban were a sight to behold. Ruthie could not get over how dangerous they looked; they were adorned in bones, shrunken skulls, garlands, and feathers from head to toe. Their faces were painted with tribal patterns, and their bodies were covered in tattoos that were relevant to their social standing. These men were Sengalang's army, his closest and most fearsome fighters, who were now preparing themselves mentally for battle against the unseen forces of darkness.

Ruthie was leaning against the trunk of one of the many dipterocarp trees that dominated this area of the jungle. Tingkar sat on her shoulder, one arm wrapped around her head. Milo and Peng sat on the ground watching in silence, only distracted by fireflies that streaked past every now and again. The cicadas joined the chorus of frogs that echoed across the valley.

The atmosphere was tense, as the night seemed ready to burst with danger.

Another rumble of thunder rolled across the horizon. A strange halo of moonlit, stormy clouds hung like a shroud over the peak of Mount Kinabalu. It was as if the mountain was readying itself.

"I hate all this waiting! Why can't we leave right now?" Ruthie finally said, breaking the silence.

"Leave for where, lah? You know the village is cut off by a curse, lah?" said a young woman in a tribal dress who was cradling a young baby.

"I don't know what's going on here, but waiting frustrates me. And where is Jim? He's got to be alive, but where did he go?" Ruthie asked in a panic. "He can't leave me now. Not with so much at stake."

"Who is this Jim you speak of, lah?"

"How can you not know?" Ruthie asked. "He's your Protector, your–" Ruthie stopped speaking when she realised the woman was gone. She felt a jolt of fear as she and the gibbons looked all around. They could find no one aside from Sengalang and the Headhunters. "Who was that woman?"

Before she could say any more, a cold wind blew across the hill, swirling like a tornado around the edge of the ancient clearing. Ruthie shivered, as within seconds each of the burning torches and the fire in the centre of the clearing became a flaming vortex reaching up into the stormy sky.

Sengalang stood at the centre of the flaming tornado, surrounded by a swarm of Headhunters, who had gone from prayer to battle-ready in seconds. Each was armed with a spear, bow and arrow, or a machete. Ruthie and the gibbons ran toward the tribesmen as the burning wall rose higher and higher, trapping them all within. Bright orange flames flared, and then were replaced by a dark, silvery mass. Swarms of shadows swirled where the fire once was, an eerie mass of cold darkness waiting to extinguish all life and light.

Sengalang raised his staff and uttered several words Ruthie could not hear above the noise. A blast of white light crackled from its tip and blasted a hole in the vortex. Swirling his staff around and around, Sengalang released a second blast of light. It zapped through the dark shadows as the lithe silhouette of a woman stalked like a ghost out of the darkness, through the wall of Headhunters, and stood defiant before Ruthie.

Ruthie's eyes went wide with recognition. Anger welled within her, and she lashed out with a punch that left her recoiling in pain as she cradled her fist. "Lady Christina! How dare you show your twisted face around here after what you did? You hurt my brother! You were supposed to be his assistant–"

"Don't even go there," the Huntress said, venom dripping from her words. "Is this better for you?"

As Ruthie watched, the Huntress morphed into a young, muscular man with a shock of reddish brown hair and a scar over his left eye. He was wearing his signature combat boots, khaki trousers and a white vest.

A pang of guilt and desire lurched through Ruthie.

"Don't you do that," Ruthie whispered. "Never do–"

"Ruthie!" Jim said, extending his hand toward her. Ruthie struggled to retain control as the image of Jim tugged at her heartstrings. A tear fell down her cheek as she looked at the man she secretly loved – and she moved to run into his arms.

Jim suddenly fell to the ground, and Ruthie snapped out of her trance. She looked down at Tingkar, who was holding a club-like branch, a worried smile on his face.

"Thank you!" she said to the gibbon, then looked around at the sea of people lying all around her. The Headhunters were helping each other, carrying the wounded away from the jungle opening and toward the longhouse. Sengalang stood next to her and put an arm on her shoulder.

"We do not stand a chance against this kind of evil. Darkness has twisted this woman as it has our mountain, lah? Let us hope the Protector is still alive…"

Sengalang signalled to two Headhunters to take the Huntress prisoner. They bound her arms and legs with thin rope, and handed the ends to Sengalang. He held them in his hands and uttered a single word: "Ikat." A flicker of light surrounded the rope, and then disappeared. As the Headhunters carried her off, Sengalang called after them.

"Guard her. Nothing or no one be safe if she gets loose…"

23. Lightning
STRIKES

"This place is like a hi-tech rabbit warren!" Rufus shouted at Jim, who was now bounding ahead in the twisting and turning corridors of the Shadowlab.

Looking back down the corridor, Rufus saw several Shadow Warriors behind them. Darkness followed them – each of the lights set into the wall blinked out as they passed.

Jim's large, hairy red hand suddenly yanked Rufus into a green-lit alcove.

"You did it, Jim!" Rufus said excitedly. "You found a way out – look at that portal!"

Jim was unsure of what he had done, but Rufus and Wira moved quickly to the monitor, bringing up the level display. Jim leaned in over Rufus' shoulder and saw a big flashing number one on the screen, as he finally comprehended where he was as he looked down at the faint metallic crop circle that was slowly filling with light.

"Is this –" Before he could complete his sentence, a blast

of vivid green light obscured Jim's vision before he and the others streaked into pixels. They re-materialised a moment later. "Where are we?"

Ahead of them was an awesome glass structure; a giant dome pierced by a lightning conductor covered in silvery black superconductor rings that grew from the darkness and rose through an opening in the roof. Rufus gasped when he saw the tubes of black slime that spread like a network covering its core.

"What are those veins?" asked Jim. He looked toward the boiling black storm clouds that swirled and grew around the needle-like point. Jim reached in his bag and removed his hockey stick, then walked toward the towering structure.

"Jim! What are you doing?" asked Rufus.

"Ending this once and for all!" He grabbed Rufus and Wira and threw them on his back.

Jim ran and leaped twenty feet into the air. He grabbed onto the structure and began to climb determinedly, making his way through the opening in the dome.

Surrounding them on all sides was an epic view of the rainforest, which had now grown dark, twisted and evil. Storm clouds rolled above. Lightning forked and thunder crashed.

Jim kept on climbing, and Rufus glanced down. With a sickly sense of vertigo as he saw a swirl of black shapes at the tower's base. They were making their way toward them. He tried shouting to get Jim's attention, but Jim already knew what was coming and was focused on only one thing. Ahead of him was a tiny platform, and Jim deposited Rufus and Wira there.

Jim continued his ascent toward the summit, passing a stack of black superconductors. The shadows swarmed up the tower, past where Rufus and Wira hid in the darkness.

Jim kept climbing, taking a quick look behind him to see the Shadow Warriors gaining on him. He looked up as a bolt of purple lightning struck the point of the tower. Electricity coursed down the black bubbling veins like neon pink snakes, through the superconductors and then through Jim!

His body went rigid, but he held onto the tower using his tattooed palm that now seemed to glow with an eerie blue light. His arm changed to human for just a second, then back to his werangutan form. Then Jim's body went limp and hung like a lifeless rag doll.

Each of the Shadow Warriors winked out of existence, overloaded by the immense power of the lightning bolt.

Rufus and Wira looked up and saw Jim's unconscious body hanging from the tower by only one hand.

✪

The bolt of electricity shot along the black veins, deeper and deeper into the Shadowlab, working its way into the heart of the Dark Matter Scope and into a tiny vial of Jim's blood. It now mutated and glowed with static energy.

A sinister laugh echoed through the Shadowlab as the electrical discharge expanded from the vial and spread into the Dark Matter Scope's ranks of black bubbling vials. The needle on the gauge slammed into the red – the danger zone and beyond. Sparks flew from the connectors as the digital screen flashed *100%*.

"Finally, I shall have my revenge!" The Shadow Emperor screamed victorious.

Doctor Gila turned toward the monitor in a panic. The black vials of Dark Matter were bubbling into such a frenzy that they shattered their glass containers. Molten black oozed from the Dark Matter Scope like blackened lava.

"What isssss happening, Gila?! I should be free!" The Shadow Emperor grew in the giant circular portal. Bit by bit, his immense form appeared. His second arm, led by razor sharp claws, reached out of the void, followed by the remainder of his giant lizard-like head. A mass of blood-red scales manifested, one by one.

Doctor Gila looked up at the giant dragon-like creature climbing through his Dark Matter Scope, and then shook his head. "What… what am I doing?" His mind was crystal clear for a single, valuable second, breaking the Shadow Emperor's hold over him. "This isn't right… Ruthie!"

"What are you doing, Gila?!" boomed the Emperor.

Gila stumbled toward the cradle of the Dark Matter Bomb. His mind was in chaos. Straining to keep control of his own thoughts, his black-gloved finger hovered and shook over a large glowing red disc.

His finger lowered onto the button – and, with a loud click, the mechanism finally released itself.

A bolt of super-charged electricity captured from the lightning strike shot down from the capacitor and into the giant electrode that hung above the Pink Pearl. Pure energy exploded into its heart, releasing a blinding white flash as the cradle moved up into the machine and disappeared inside.

"What… what have we *done*?" whispered Gila.

"No, Gila – it was *you*! *You* dragged me here; *you* have instigated the destruction of your world. The weight of the guilt will smother you… enhance you… make you more powerful!"

"Noooooo!" Doctor Gila fell to his knees, his hands clapped against his head. His mind felt ready to burst. "I can't…"

"Don't resist its power – embrace it!"

"Aaaarrgghhhh!" Gila contorted in pain as the Shadow Emperor continued to crawl out of the void. As Gila looked up through his remaining eye, he felt a tear fall down his cheek. He cried out as he tried to reach the gauge's emergency pressure release.

"Noooooooooooooooooooooooo!" screamed the Shadow Emperor, but before he could stop Doctor Gila, the scientist pulled at the lever with all his remaining strength. The Dark Matter Scope screamed as vents expelled steaming jets of black. The pressure levels rose as hundreds of Dark Matter vials exploded, bubbling over him like a fountain of pure evil.

Gila didn't stand a chance. The last thing he saw was the pressure gauge finally plummeting to zero.

A howl of anguish came from the Shadow Emperor as he found his path into the universe suddenly and brutally blocked.

Half emerged from the portal was the front half of an immense red dragon, its wings unfurled in fury – trapped between worlds.

An ear-piercing and scorching roar of fire bellowed from the jaws of the Shadow Emperor as he reached over with a giant clawed hand and slammed the launch button of the Dark Matter Bomb.

"If I cannot be in this world, I will dessstroy it!" The Shadow Emperor roared in fury as he saw the Dark Matter drain into the floor below the machine, along with the remains of Doctor Gila.

24. Ascent to
MOUNT KINABALU

The storm was fierce, flashing over the horizon and growing angrier with each passing minute. Rufus and Wira were sitting on the maintenance platform, huddled under a piece of plastic tarpaulin. They could barely see Jim's prone form above them, so blinding was the rain. The wind picked up, making the tarpaulin flap and billow like a sail.

"Jim! Jim!" Rufus shouted above the din.

When Jim didn't stir, Rufus knew what he had to do. He reached out and grabbed the cold, rain-slicked metal of the tower and started to climb. Slow and determined, he edged his way toward Jim, the rain soaking him to the bone. Rufus kept climbing, letting his adrenaline take over, until finally, he reached Jim.

He grabbed the duffle bag that still hung around Jim's neck, pulling it closer to him. He tried shaking Jim but there was no response. Then he noticed the Headhunter Skull glowing. As Rufus touched the skull, its voice echoed in his mind.

"*You can save him! Have faith in the Orang-eee!*"

Rufus closed his eyes and kept his hand gripped tight on the skull. A strange tingling shot through Rufus' fingers and up into his arms, then spread throughout his entire body. He reached out for Jim but lost his grip on the wet metal of the tower and he started to fall.

A giant hand swooped out of nowhere and pulled him to safety. He was staring his best friend in the face, Jim's giant eyes reflecting Rufus' fear-flushed expression.

"Jimbo! I thought you were *dead!*"

The werangutan's piercing blue eyes were full of fire and determination. "You know me, Rufus! I wouldn't let a little thing like death get in the way of an *epic rescue!*"

Rufus stuffed the skull back into Jim's duffle bag, as Jim started to move them back to the small platform next to Wira. The orangutan was already climbing up the tower to meet them. Before they got halfway down they saw a blinding pink light coursing up the centre of the tower.

"What *is* that?" shouted Jim.

"Oh no," said Rufus in panic. "The Dark Matter Bomb!"

"The *what?*"

Jim grabbed Wira and launched into the air in pursuit of the pink light. He leapt into the night, grabbing the bottom of the missile with his tattooed hand as it flew past. Jim was amazed at how sharp and acute his reflexes had become, even more than his days as a top ice hockey star. His grip was sure and solid, and even though his arm felt like it might be pulled from its socket, he felt completely in control.

The trio rocketed into the night, blasting through the eye of the tower one by one in a long train, toward the summit of the mountain.

Jim, Rufus, and Wira screamed at the top of their lungs when the bomb changed direction, slowly arcing toward the swirling mists of the mysterious Lowes Peak.

Without warning, a spherical force field grew out of the cradle like a giant bubble, surrounding the bomb and its trio of hangers-on. The cradle holding the missile and the Pink Pearl crashed to earth – into a crater blasted out of solid granite.

"Ouch!" Jim lifted himself off the ground and onto his knees, gasping for the air that had been knocked out of his lungs on impact.

"Look at the view!" Rufus exclaimed, standing dazed and bedraggled in the torrential rain. "Not a scratch!" he said as Wira leapt onto his shoulders and gave him a thumbs-up. They both stood in awe, looking into the wilderness of black rolling clouds that sprawled below them. Way below they glimpsed rainforest as far as the eye could see... although it was now dark and menacing, a twisted phantom-like version of Borneo mutated by the Dark Matter leeching into its roots and leaves.

Jim straightened himself and looked toward the centre

of the crater. Therein lay the bomb attached to the Pink Pearl, a countdown clock glowing in the half-light: *0024* – and it was steadily counting down.

"Quick!" shouted Jim, grabbing his bag and sweeping Rufus and Wira off their feet, throwing them behind a granite peak.

0003…

He covered them both with his large body.

0002…

In the last second he grabbed the Headhunter Skull, holding it tight against his forehead.

0001…

0000.

The numbers blinked twice and then the world went white.

BOOM!

✪

Outside the Iban Headhunters' longhouse, under a corrugated metal lean-to, Ruthie repacked her bag, surrounded by five of her remaining gibbons. A pair of chickens clucked and scratched at the ground, completely unconcerned that the end of the world was just a few pecks away.

She heard footsteps behind her.

"Lady, we wish you all good luck," said Sengalang, who was approaching with two armed Headhunters. "You will–"

Before Sengalang could finish, an old air raid siren sounded across the jungle. Moments later a blinding white light blasted from the peak of Mount Kinabalu, followed by a sonic boom that shook the ground.

Ruthie and the gibbons covered their eyes, protecting themselves from the cloud of white fire that was heading toward the village, evaporating everything in its path.

Thinking quickly, Sengalang threw Ruthie to the ground as the fireball swept across the village. He felt the heat – but then realised with a cry of relief that the curse encircling the Iban village also *protected* it. The heat and light was intense, but they were alive!

✪

The jungle, however, continued to burn. The devastation was all-consuming. Trees flared like matchsticks. Villagers and local tribes-people tried to outrun the firestorm but failed. Flocks of giant hornbills took flight but were turned into clouds of ash – instant death.

Nothing could survive.

✪

As the shock wave spread from the centre of the bomb, the ground shook and Mount Kinabalu shuddered. The Shadow Emperor was pleased – until he saw the computer monitors flicker and die. The laboratory lights sparked and then extinguished. A large electro-magnetic pulse bounced through the system, deep into the heart of the Shadowlab.

Way below, on Level 666, the Dark Matter Reactor shook. The lava pools that now surrounded the immense machine bubbled and rippled, then surged forward like a tidal wave, swamping the reactor unit. Emergency lights flickered on, illuminating a large red light below the reactor monitor. *Shielding Offline: Danger*, it read.

The ground shook again as the Earth's crust shifted, ejecting a giant plume of lava from its core, spewing through the vents on the sides of the granite peak of the mountain. The mists of Lowes Gully now glowed like hot amber in the night as all the moisture in the air steamed away.

✪

Jim, Rufus, and Wira dared to look down as a deafening rumble came from below. A vast army of Dark Shadow Warriors swirled up from the depths of the mountain. Jim held Rufus and Wira in a hairy red bear hug.

Rufus shook with fear and sadness. He could see that the island of Borneo was burning, turning slowly into a blackened pile of burning rock that bled flaming red lava.

"How could this have happened?" he asked, choking on the heat and ash. "Look at the death and destruction, the irresponsibility…"

"Do you think it will spread beyond the island?" Jim asked, staring out of the bubble.

The flames receded, as an eerie pink mushroom cloud

bloomed in the sky. The ground shook once more as the side of the mountain started to splinter off into Lowes Gully.

The power of the explosion combined with the Dark Matter until it reached critical mass. A giant swirling orb of silvery black rose from the burning depths of the gully. The trio stared in fear as it bubbled and grew bigger and bigger, like an obsidian mirror, absorbing the energy of the explosion.

Then it burst.

There in the sky was a giant, dragon-like creature of unspeakable monstrousness. Its eyes glowed with a mystical white fire as its giant black leathery wings unfurled like a giant bat.

It moved closer to where Jim, Rufus, and Wira lay, opening its mouth to reveal razor sharp teeth, its arms reaching out to grasp them with long silver claws.

"Wild Man!" came the voice from the Headhunter Skull. "The powers of the Orang-eee have protected you!"

"Sengalang, is that you?" Jim asked, holding the skull in front of him.

"Wild Man, I must be quick! Some kind of force field has surrounded the village for some time, but it is slowly disintegrating since the explosion, lah. This evil needs to be stopped, now! Its reign must come to an end. With our combined forces we will extinguish this darkness together."

"Sengalang!" Jim shouted, "Sengalang!" The skull had gone silent.

"Where did he go?" asked Rufus in a panic.

Suddenly the skull levitated into the air above the trio, and the black dragon-beast rose from the fire, roaring in anger.

Orange light emanated from the skull and surrounded the group – then a funnel-like tube of whirling light blasted through the protective bubble and shot up into the night sky arcing down into the jungle below.

"What is it doing, Jim?"

"I haven't got a clue, Rufus, but it seems to have opened some sort of portal or something…"

Before Jim could say any more, several Headhunters landed on the ground next to them, followed by Sengalang, Ruthie and the five gibbons. As they got to their feet and regrouped, Jim noticed that they now had a whole army of Headhunters with them, armed to the teeth with machetes, blowpipes, bows and arrows.

As the force field began to disintegrate, Sengalang's tribal army readied themselves to take on the giant Dark Matter dragon that now ruled the sky. The beast let out a deafening roar. A sonic blast hit them shaking them where they stood.

For a terrifying instant Jim looked up at the creature. Their eyes met and Jim felt a kind of connection.

It was as though they had met before…

"Who are y...?" Jim mouthed in the confusion.

"*Hahahhahahahhaaaaaa!*"

"Gila?" Jim whispered. "How did you survive?"

There was a fizzing crackle as the skull's force field flickered and disappeared. The band of heroes prepared for the dragon to strike.

The battle was just beginning.

25. The Battle for
BORNEO

Within seconds of the force field failing, a horde of Shadow Warriors appeared and moved in to attack. Jim stood next to Ruthie and Rufus, the three of them defiant. Wira sat on Rufus' shoulders, ready for battle. The Headhunters fell into line behind the three heroes as Sengalang stepped forward across the blackened granite that now hissed with heat. Thin rivulets of molten orange rock ran like veins across the blackened surface. Sengalang looked determined as he raised his staff in the air.

"Leave this place! You are not welcome! Go back to your world and stay there!" Sengalang's voice boomed louder and stronger than Jim had ever heard it. Both armies seemed to be waiting for the right moment to attack.

Thunder rumbled then crackled above them as a bolt of angry purple lightning blew a crater into the granite rock between the two massed forces. They shielded their eyes as rock and glowing embers filled the air like tiny orbs of burning gold.

The explosion triggered action, as Sengalang charged the Dark Shadow army, with Jim right behind him. The shaman fired several concentric circles of white light from his staff toward the line of Shadow Warriors that had gathered beneath the Dark Matter Dragon.

The Headhunters ran into the fray and clashed with the Shadow Warriors, their machetes slashing and arrows flying through the air.

Rufus ran across the rocky mountain peak, Wira following close behind him. Wira picked up something small and metal and threw it to Rufus. Rufus caught it and turned it over in his hands, recognising it as a Dark Matter Blaster, similar to the ones he saw in the Shadowlab near the Dark Matter Scope.

"You sneaky little..." exclaimed Rufus as he beamed with admiration for his new friend.

He felt enthralled, invigorated with this piece of luck now in his hand, but was not ready as he tripped on a rock and fell. The momentum made him roll over himself, across the rock and come up into a kneeling position. His arms were outstretched like a secret agent as he fired off two blasts from the pistol at the approaching shadows that instantly blinked out of existence.

"How cool is that?" Rufus exclaimed, high-fiving Wira. "Game on!"

✪

From behind the ranks of Shadow Warriors emerged a whole new problem. A horde of monstrous, mutated creatures swarmed up from the depths, set free by the explosions and cracks in the Shadowlab.

Giant insects fluttered like armour-plated gunships, while two mutated elephants covered in spikes stomped their way across the lava-veined granite toward a line of Headhunters. The Iban soldiers retaliated by throwing spears dipped in poison.

The earth shook as an elephant reared back on its hind legs, trumpeting its call of pain as the poison took hold. It stumbled wildly, knocking into its partner, and they both fell to the ground with a crash.

A chittering hiss came from the side of the mountain, and the Headhunters knew something even more hideous was coming toward them…

A swarm of giant black and yellow spiders came into view, their armour shining in the firelight and liquid web shooting from their clicking mandibles. Several Headhunters became trapped in the web and were instantly pounced on.

✪

Sengalang looked on as the battle raged, focusing on the giant dragon-like creature. It was still hanging there menacingly as it commanded the mutated creatures to do its bidding. Sengalang was repulsed and saddened by the noble jungle creatures that had been warped by the insidious Dark Matter.

"We are all creatures of this earth, but you cannot be allowed to destroy what I have come to love. *Bakar!*" he shouted, raising his staff. A wall of flame shot from the staff's glowing tip toward the spiders, incinerating them before more Headhunters perished. The bombardment of creatures and Shadow Warriors was taking its toll on the Iban army, but they fought on relentlessly.

✪

Jim came to an opening in the melée and stood at his full height, roaring in defiance. A bright light caught his attention, and he looked toward the dragon that loomed above him. Beneath its razor-clawed foot was a glowing orb – the Pink Pearl! Although the bomb's machinery had been destroyed, the heart remained intact, and was now levitating and pulsating with energy. Jim knew the only way to end this was to destroy the pearl.

He felt renewed energy course through him, flowing through his veins. It was the feeling he used to get before an ice-hockey game. It was this fire that burned deep within that gave him the nickname of "Jungle Jim." It was a power and energy that enhanced his senses and gave him a new level of hope. He drew his hockey stick and stood ready for the final attack.

Ruthie, meanwhile, charged into a line of Shadow

Warriors, armed with her two pistols and flanked on either side by her band of gibbons. Next to her, a small team of hunters raised their blowpipes and blew a wave of darts toward a wall of darkness. Each of the darts was imbued with Iban magic, and the Shadow Warriors flickered and fizzled into nothingness.

Jim grabbed a Shadow Warrior with both hands, throwing it into several more until they tumbled away in a twisted mass. He made his way toward Ruthie, who was now staring at the dragon.

Ruthie couldn't move from her spot as she stared at the glowing eyes of the dragon. Its giant mouth was open, revealing its silvery white fangs. Its eyes seemed to bore right into Ruthie, searching and reaching into her…

Hahahahahahahahaha!

All Ruthie could hear was the cackle of laughter as her vision flashed white and her head exploded in pain. She grabbed her head with both hands; her eyes squeezed shut as visions flickered inside her head. She saw her brother Albert in his science lab, his expression of excitement as he poured over a monitor display, surrounded by glass vats of thick, bubbling black slime. She saw a face of pure evil in the darkness: the Shadow Emperor laughing, then an explosion. She saw her brother amidst all the damage, wounded and in pain – then he changed and she saw the creature he became.

Her eyes opened as the fog in her head cleared and everything fell into place. She looked at the creature in front of her and, suddenly, she recognised it.

"Albert," she whispered. "It's you… what have you done?" Tears streamed down her cheeks.

The monster that was once Albert Moo reared up in anger and let out a terrible roar. It lowered its head toward its sister and her gibbons and unleashed a lethal blast of Dark Matter fire.

26. The Cost of
VICTORY

Sengalang saw what was happening from afar, and he fired a protective shield from his staff that encircled Ruthie. The fire billowed all around her but did not touch her. Ruthie shielded her eyes as the gibbons clung to her legs. Enraged, the Dark Matter dragon covered the mountain in a sweeping arc of fire. Headhunters and Shadow Warriors evaporated in the blast as the creature let loose its fury.

Rufus and Wira watched from behind a white-hot boulder as Jim charged toward the glowing object beneath the dragon's foot. *The Pink Pearl*, thought Rufus.

Standing with his feet firmly planted apart, Rufus raised his Dark Matter blaster in both hands and pulled the trigger, firing at the dragon's foot. The first blast did nothing but irritate the creature, but after ten blasts it writhed in pain and released its grip on the pearl.

"Thanks Rufus!" said Jim as he removed his lucky hockey puck from his duffle bag and kissed it. "Just one more time for me, okay?" Using his superhuman strength, he flicked it with perfect precision into the air, and then used his hockey stick to send it hurtling toward the pearl.

Sengalang and the others watched as the world seemed to slip into slow motion. The ancient Pink Pearl glowed intensely one last time – and then the puck slammed into it, shattering it into a million crystalline pieces. The Iban shaman felt a glimmer of hope, as the creature immediately shrank in size.

"Yes!" Jim shouted, raising his hockey stick in the air. Before the creature could recover, Jim charged the Dark Matter monster like an angry bull. He lowered his shoulders and rammed into the black dragon, toppling it over the edge. It lost its balance and plunged into the abyss of Lowes Gully.

Jim could not stop his own momentum, and he fell forward, his weight tumbling him into the gully and the mists below.

"Noooooooo!" Rufus screamed, watching his best friend fall from sight. He turned and fired the Dark Matter Blaster at the remaining Shadow Warriors. They were easy to pick off – the loss of the Pink Pearl made them weaker as they dwindled in number.

Shouting one last ancient Iban curse at the remaining Shadow Warriors, Sengalang used his staff to wipe them from the earth. He felt no relief from their victory, just great sadness at the loss of their great Protector.

Ruthie fell to her knees and shouted Jim's name, but she knew he was gone. Silence descended on the mountain top. Moonlight shone from behind the clouds, bathing the survivors in a cold light.

Their world had been destroyed and their Protector and friend was gone.

Nothing remained but a fire-blasted wasteland.

✪

The Huntress stirred. The Headhunter village was quiet and empty. Her wrists hurt, and she looked down to see them bound by rope. The more she moved the more pain she felt, and she realised the rope was no ordinary rope.

"Iban magic!" she spat. She looked around her and noticed the longhouse and its surrounding area were undamaged, but beyond it all was a smouldering blackness. "The jungle! It can't have actually *worked*?" she muttered.

Doctor Gila must have detonated the Dark Matter Bomb, she thought. And then she felt the Shadow Emperor burning into her mind.

"Master!" she cried, then realised he was in danger. Her body contorted and her eyes flared yellow as she screamed in pain – the ropes that bound her wrists were growing tighter. Then, in a moment of pure anger and hatred, she transformed into a yellow mist and evaporated, having overpowered the Iban magic.

27. The Naked
TRUTH

Rufus and Ruthie couldn't believe their friend was gone. The sadness lay on them like a heavy blanket as the remaining group of Iban Headhunters drew together and gathered around Sengalang.

"We have lost our Protector, our saviour, our friend," said the old man mournfully. "We must be strong in this time of darkness, lah. We must not take our eyes from the evil or it will take hold once more."

Rufus put his arm around Ruthie to comfort her as Wira wrapped his long hairy arms around both their legs in a hug. Suddenly Wira stiffened and looked around, sniffing the air. Unwrapping his arms from Rufus and Ruthie, he ambled carefully toward the edge of Lowes Gully.

The jagged gash in the earth was deep and foreboding, but the thick mist that hung in the air prevented Wira from seeing much. He peeked over the edge of the mountain, careful to keep himself from slipping or falling over. Ruthie joined him.

"Be careful!" Rufus warned her. "Don't get too close to the edge." They all sat in silence, paying their last respects to their fallen comrade.

Wira suddenly perked up, and then jumped onto Rufus' shoulders. "What is it, Wira?" asked Rufus. He felt someone behind him and turned to see Sengalang and the Headhunters standing there, a small smile on the shaman's face.

"Don't give up on your friend just yet. The winds are changing…"

He waved his long bony hand and muttered something under his breath. The mists swirled as a gentle breeze cleared them away to reveal a scene of epic devastation. It was a vision of hell.

Ruthie suddenly widened her eyes in surprise. She grabbed Rufus' arm and pointed – and his mouth fell open.

"Well, what are you all waiting for?" came a familiar voice from below.

"Jim!" yelled Rufus in delight. "You're alive!"

"And human! And naked!" added Ruthie, as she watched Jim hanging from the end of a tree root.

"Don't just stand there gawping at me, help me! It's freezing down here!"

Sengalang looked down at Jim with a smile, his eyes twinkling in the night.

Tingkar slapped a hand over Ruthie's eyes. She pushed

the gibbon's hand away and peered out at Jim, who was hanging by one arm and using the other to cover himself in an act of modesty. A wave of happiness and relief flooded through her as she finally accepted that this was the Jim she knew and loved. "It really *is* you!" she said.

"Yes, I know that! I told you it was *me* all along. Now will someone help me up before I fall again or freeze to death?"

Several Headhunters lowered a length of rope over the edge. Jim looked up at the group, and then cleared his throat.

"Uh, would you all mind looking the other way?"

Everyone but Ruthie turned around; she still couldn't believe what she was seeing. Rufus noticed and spun her so that she was now facing away from Jim as he began climbing the rope.

Once Jim had clambered to safety, he opened his duffle bag and quickly took out a small towel to cover himself. He saw Sengalang pick up his lucky hockey puck from the pulverized remains of the Pink Pearl, which now glistened like tiny grains of crystal in the moonlight.

Sengalang looked at the hockey puck, turning it over in his hands. He saw where it read 'The Stroke of Luck' and he chuckled. "So true, so true." He handed it back to Jim. He then bent and picked up a few pieces of the Pink Pearl. He held a bigger piece up to the moon, studying it and smiling when the light shone through the fragment onto his face. He spoke some sacred words under his breath and threw the shard onto the ashes that were still glowing faintly from the lava.

Jim, now covered in an Iban blanket, looked over at Sengalang, who seemed to be aglow in the soft light of the moon. As he watched the light got brighter and brighter, then so bright it hurt his eyes. He tried to shield them, as did the others, but it was no use.

The small shard of the Pink Pearl sparked into life, blinding and bright absorbing the flame and lava caused by the Dark Matter Bomb. Reality seemed to warp, spin backward, and then warp again as the light got brighter and brighter like the birth of a new star.

The jungle that had been decimated by the Shadow Emperor now came back to life. Tiny green shoots burst through the charred earth and spread at an incredibly fast rate, and soon there was once again green covering the land as far as the eye could see. The jungle was regenerating; a tidal wave of lushness rushing up Mount Kinabalu and restoring what was damaged.

Sengalang held up the new Pink Pearl as the Headhunters bowed in front of it in prayer. The shaman smiled and spoke.

"From death and destruction a new pearl, greater than the one before, shall rise from the flames. Arise! Arise!

Our Protector has saved us!"

The ball of crackling energy around the Pink Pearl expanded and absorbed a tiny bit of life force from those who had witnessed its re-creation. Pink light danced about, then the pearl was whole and reborn.

✪

"Life on this island will start anew," said Jim, looking out at the green jungle. "For the better, free of darkness and shadows."

"That remains to be seen, Wild Man," said Sengalang. "But first, we must save you from overexposure!" He winked at Jim and gathered the Headhunters around him.

Jim looked down at himself. "I'm human again?" he said. "I can't believe it."

Ruthie walked over to Jim and winked. "Bit cold, isn't it, Wild Man? I think we should get you warm and dressed."

Rufus reached into Jim's duffle bag and retrieved the Headhunter Skull, holding it up for Jim to see. "I think we're going to need this, yes?"

Sengalang placed the Pink Pearl onto a plinth of black granite at the pinnacle of the mountain, then turned and twirled his right hand, his index finger outstretched. A swirl of orange mist emanated from the skull and grew like a tornado, taking hold of everyone. The group evaporated in the orange mists, and dissipated as the skull disappeared with a loud pop!

✪

Deep beneath the mountain, Level 666 of the Shadowlab was a different story. Lava bubbled and swelled, and mini eruptions shook the ground around the Dark Matter Reactor. A red warning light glowed, echoing the orangey-red glow of the lava that was welling up from the centre of the Earth's core. The Shadowlab shook, then a giant crack opened across the floor. Things were going to get worse.

In another part of the lab, a small emergency light flickered on, casting a faint glow across the blood-red scales of the Shadow Emperor. Large eyelids flickered open, revealing eyes ablaze with evil inner light.

"I will desssstroy thisss planet and take its blasted Protector with it! These pitiful humanssss shall regret ever trying to sssstop me! *Hahahahahahahahahaha…*"

28.

FREEDOM

"I don't think I'll ever get used to this kind of travel!" shouted Rufus as he fell on top of Jim.

Jim rolled aside and knocked into Ruthie, who looked as queasy and disoriented as Rufus. "It's certainly a unique way of getting around, I'll admit," she added.

Another swirling maelstrom of orange mist appeared above the boardwalk of Kampong Ayer, and the scorched jetty planks soon creaked under the weight of a large group of Iban Headhunters. Several others fell out of the vortex and right into the river with a confused splash.

"I think we need to iron out a few kinks for sure," said Jim, laughing at the mess of people, monkeys and Iban weapons.

"Let's get cleaned up!" said Ruthie. "Then I think it's time to celebrate – if *The Moody Cow* is still open for business!"

✪

The Moody Cow was crowded with locals. Skinny men dressed in tattered shorts and T-shirts mixed with ladies in sarongs, who all mingled with a large group of celebrating Iban Headhunters. The Tuak was free flowing, its milky white liquid scorching the throats of the locals.

Ruthie's gibbons sat on their own special shelves, looking down on the room from above. The main area was lit by fireflies in jars, which cast the room with a warm green glow.

In pride of place at the back of the bar stood a giant dark-wood jukebox marked with the name Shenanigans, playing old vinyl records of 1950s and 1960s classics. The mood was jubilant.

At the centre of the bar stood Jim, clad once again in his signature boots, khaki trousers and a brand-new white vest. Next to him stood Rufus, his hair immaculately styled, taking large sips of Tuak.

"Whooo!" Rufus exclaimed as he swallowed the liquid and coughed.

"Whoa there, take it easy," said Jim, patting his friend on the back.

"That'll put hairs on your chest," Ruthie said from behind the bar. She was drying glasses and enjoying herself. "It might even finally make a man of you!"

After coughing some more, Rufus turned to her in exasperation. "After all that we've been through you still have doubts?"

As she laughed warmly, Jim couldn't take his eyes off of

Ruthie. She stood tall and lithe, her hair swept back in a long ponytail. Her face beamed, but there was still sadness in her eyes.

"What is it?" asked Jim.

"Oh, its nothing."

"Tell me," he pressed. "Is it Albert? I'm so sorry about what happened, Ruthie…"

"I just can't believe all those things he did. What he became…"

"Don't, Ruthie. Think of the here and now. His experiments may have caused a lot of damage and harm, but he's gone now, and there's so much good to focus on…"

"We survived!" interrupted Rufus. "We're alive, and *you*, Wild Man, are human again. There's a lot to celebrate!"

Ruthie smiled at Rufus' words. "That's true. I'm glad you're the Jim Regent I know and –"

"Would you come back to England with me?" interrupted Jim, desperate to know her answer.

She lowered her head, avoiding his gaze. "Jim… I can't. I have work here. I work for the British government; I can't just give that up. And besides, I think Albert is still alive. I felt it on top of the mountain. He's somewhere out there, and he needs me. I have to find my brother and bring him back home…" She broke off, crying, and buried her face in Jim's chest. He held her tight, not saying a word. "I love you," she finally whispered, then broke his hug and walked to the back room.

Jim sighed. He glanced around the room, looking for Rufus. At least he could turn to his best friend for support and some wise words. His gaze fell on an aristocratic-looking man in crisp khakis and wearing a monocle. He stared back at Jim, smoothing his yellowing handlebar moustache. He then returned to his copy of the *Screams of the Six O'Clock Cicada* newspaper, its headline boldly stating: "Man-beast spotted in Kampong Ayer!" Jim was too late to divert his eyes, as he had made eye contact with the mysterious man, who was lurking in the corner behind a swathe of smoke. Jim groaned at the headline and decided it was time to leave.

✪

Outside, the air was stirred by a warm, gentle breeze that seemed to blow right from the newly healed Mount Kinabalu. The insects chirped their usual night song, and everything seemed normal to Jim as he walked over to Sengalang, who stood looking at the black waters that reflected the midnight sky above.

"There's no moon this evening," Jim said to the shaman, who turned his sad eyes to face him. "Have you got it hidden somewhere?"

Sengalang reached into his little pouch and withdrew a shiny band of white gold. He extended it to Jim, who whistled his appreciation. "It's beautiful."

"What did you expect, Wild Man? We are not all savages, you know!"

"I didn't mean…"

I know," chuckled Sengalang. "I am only pulling your leg. This ring belonged to my wife. Now it will belong to you."

"What?" Jim replied in shock. "I can't take this, it's—"

"Enough! I have grown to think of you as a son. All these years I have watched you grow and become a man. The young man you are today, standing here before me. My wife is gone, like your parents, but she would wish for me to give this to someone I deem worthy."

Jim was silent as he looked at Sengalang. This wise man thought him an equal? Thought him worthy?

"Are you sure?" Jim finally asked.

"I would not offer this precious gift if I did not wish to. You are our great Protector." Sengalang took Jim's hand and placed the ring in his palm. Jim felt great warmth as he closed his hand around it.

"Thank you, Sengalang," Jim said, and before he realised what he was doing he grabbed the old man and gave him a big hug. "You've become like a father and mentor to me…"

Sengalang tried to extricate himself from Jim, who was embarrassed and straightened Sengalang's robes for him. The shaman smiled at Jim and patted his cheek. "You are welcome, Wild Man." Then he turned and walked back to the bar.

Jim watched him go, then after a few more minutes of silent contemplation, he too returned to the snug and friendly atmosphere of *The Moody Cow*.

Rufus saw Jim walk back into *The Moody Cow* and signalled for his best friend to join him. Jim smiled and held up a finger to let Rufus know he would join him in a minute.

He moved toward the bar on a mission. Ruthie saw Jim approach and smiled at him. Jim took the ring from his trouser pocket and moved toward her, his expression one of hope and joy. He knew what he had to do.

Suddenly he felt queasy, his head pounded as a wave of nausea swept over him. Jim looked down and saw what looked like a giant sleeping orangutan. "What?" he said as he shook his head to clear it. He blinked, and then realised that the orangutan was just a local who had fallen asleep on the floor. He moved to step over the man but tripped instead, falling right into Ruthie's arms.

"Whoa!"

"Talk about throwing yourself at at a girl," laughed Ruthie playfully as she struggled to hold Jim's weight.

Jim tried to stand but couldn't, and he dropped to one knee, all the strength in his legs gone.

A strange orange light suddenly seemed to blast through the slats of the windows in the bar, blinding everyone. Ruthie looked down at Jim in fear and confusion as she saw the glint of metal on the wooden floor beneath Jim's open hand.

"Aaaaaaarrrgghhh!" Jim screamed in pain, gripping his head with both hands. It felt like fire coursing through his veins, burning his body from within. His eyes felt like they were going to pop out of his head as the pressure intensified. Rufus rushed over to join them, and both he and Ruthie looked at their friend helplessly as he writhed in pain on the floor.

"Jim!" Ruthie screamed as she watched Jim's body convulse, a crowd now forming around them. Jim's trousers tore as his legs grew in thickness, followed by his boots, which burst open as his feet grew to several times their normal size. His hands balled into fists as his body enlarged and was quickly covered in thick orange fur. The tattoo on his bicep burned bright – he had become the werangutan once more!

From the other side of the bar, the mysterious monocled man grabbed a large blunderbuss rifle from underneath his table and slowly walked toward Jim, who was now glowing with blinding orange light as the crowd inside the bar stampeded for the exit.

Ruthie picked the ring up from the floor and grabbed Rufus' hand in shock. She looked down at the ring in her hand and squeezed it tight.

✪

Sengalang stood outside the bar, soaking up the orange light and listened to the chaos within.

"The Rite of the Orange Moon," he chuckled. "Welcome back, Wild Man."

A crowd of people charged out of The Moody Cow, screaming in panic. Seconds later the door flew off its hinges. In the doorway stood a hulking eight-foot-tall mutant orangutan. Leaping onto the jetty, Jim the werangutan roared at the orange moon, baring his animal fangs.

Ruthie and Rufus emerged from the bar, looking at Sengalang for answers.

"I fear there is some unfinished business to attend to," he said calmly. "As long as his destiny as Protector of the Iban Headhunters remains unfulfilled, our Wild Man won't be going home just yet…"

The End?

N.B. No people or animals (or big mutated bugs) were harmed in the writing of this book.

Jungle Jim will return in...

About the
AUTHOR

James King aka 'Jungle Jim', is a writer, designer and photographer with a passion for adventure. Over the past 17 years he has been lucky enough to have travelled to many a far-flung place. From the moment he landed head-first in the Borneo rainforest, he knew he wanted to see the great wonders of the world, from the 'lost' city of Machu Picchu to the ancient temples of Angkor. He has flown over the Nazca Lines, gazed in awe at the Forbidden City, crossed the Great Wall of China, stood in the burning sands of the Erg Chebbi dunes, been shipwrecked on a dilapidated Costa Rican jungle prison island over run by howler monkeys, walked across fire and finally negotiated the notoriously perilous London Underground journey from Liverpool Street Station to Tottenham Court Road on the Central Line (at rush hour) more times than any man alive.

Life has led him in many directions, work-wise, and has been lucky enough to set foot in Skywalker Ranch and visit that 'Galaxy far, far away....' while working on *The Official Star Wars Fact File*. He has also travelled in time with *Doctor Who - Battles in Time* magazine and the *Doctor Who DVD Files*, and splashed around in the sewers of New York designing a highly successful Teenage Mutant Ninja Turtles trading card magazine for the Russian markets. All of these experiences allowed his mind to run riot and create exciting concepts and ideas for magazines aimed at younger readers.

✪

It was only a matter of time before he realised his destiny was to combine all he had learnt from this experience and make something of his own wild ideas.

He has taken inspiration from the people he met and the places he has visited, the mythology and local legends surrounding his own experiences of surviving in the darkest depths of the Borneo rainforest. The three-month expedition to Brunei and Sabah, with Raleigh International, in 1998 allowed him to jump in the deep end and experience a life that many would never get to see. Taking his diary and a love of ancient civilisations he evolved them into the fictional story of '*Jungle Jim and the Shadows of Kinabalu*'; the beginning of an epic adventure that mixes ancient mythology with a little monster bashing madness, topped off with a little sparkle of magic to save the world, as we know it, from total destruction.

CPSIA information can be obtained
at www.ICGtesting.com
Printed in the USA
LVOW01s0210121215
466395LV00033B/1616/P